# Finding Home

## A Parable of Kingdom Life

by

Brad Huebert

iUniverse, Inc.
New York   Bloomington

*Finding Home*
*A Parable of Kingdom Life*

This is a work of fiction. All of the characters, names, incidents, organizations, and dialogue in this novel are either the products of the author's imagination or are used fictitiously.

iUniverse books may be ordered through booksellers or by contacting:

iUniverse
1663 Liberty Drive
Bloomington, IN 47403
www.iuniverse.com
1-800-Authors (1-800-288-4677)

Because of the dynamic nature of the Internet, any Web addresses or links contained in this book may have changed since publication and may no longer be valid. The views expressed in this work are solely those of the author and do not necessarily reflect the views of the publisher, and the publisher hereby disclaims any responsibility for them.

ISBN: 978-0-595-51778-7 (pbk)
ISBN: 978-0-595-50720-7 (cloth)
ISBN: 978-0-595-62028-9 (ebk)

Printed in the United States of America

*To Paul and Kevin: True brothers and citizens of the realm*
*"Seek first the kingdom of God" (Matthew 6:33).*

Also by Brad Huebert:
*Take the Plunge: Journey into Prayer*

# Contents

# Foreword

There are times when what we've seen through a "glass darkly" becomes vivid and clear. Reading *Finding Home* was one of those experiences of illumination for me. Brad Huebert has invited us into a new understanding of the joy, freedom and grace of the kingdom through the doorway of our imagination. For followers of the King who are tired of books like "10 Keys to This" or "15 Principles to Achieve That," this story will both entertain and inspire.

Despite the multitude of resources supporting spiritual growth in the West, the Church seems to have limited impact on culture. Working harder and doing more isn't helping. Perhaps we need a new starting point. A new definition of how we enjoy relationship with God. A focus on being rather than doing.

The truths in this book have percolated through Brad's spiritual journey, his family relationships, and his discipleship impact as a pastor. Brad's feet are firmly planted in the truth of God's word and his heart is alive with passion for God. He has lived this story. So can we.

*Randy Friesen*
General Director
MBMS International

# Acknowledgments

So many people have helped *Finding Home* find its way into print. Thank you, Mom and Dad Huebert—you believed in me since the moment I arrived on this planet and have proven it through patience, prayers, finances, and lifelong encouragement in this dream; Brian and Sonia Huebert, the support and finances for this project have been invaluable; Mom and Dad Warkentin, Mark and Neena Huebert—your love and prayers have been critical; Tim Geddert—I asked you for your time and received a glowing endorsement, great feedback, and much-appreciated help beyond the call of duty; Randy Friesen—you modeled a kingdom life with Jesus squarely on the throne in your heart at a time when I needed to see it plain as day, and you wrote me a great foreword; Dalhousie Community Church, my church family—you have blessed me to be who I am and have seen writing as an exciting part of my pastoral ministry; Kevin Miller—you helped me see that the manuscript wasn't working as non-fiction; Kevin Geddert—you tell me the truth about my writing (what a gift!); Shauna—you are my warrior princess, my greatest fan, my wife for life, my best friend, my partner in ministry; Noah, Glory, and Joel, my incredible children—you put up with me working on my laptop between hikes and sword battles and butterfly kisses at night, and bring such joy to my heart; and finally my King—you are the magnificent Lord God Almighty, my one and only Savior who breathes life into me every single day. You are worthy of all my love and fealty in this life and the next.

# Introduction

Bone-headed disciple that I am, I arm-wrestled this confounded manuscript for eight years before figuring out why I couldn't seem to pin it to the table.

It's a book about the kingdom of heaven.

See, when Jesus taught about his kingdom, he shunned traditional outlines. He never hammered out a distended seminary thesis or punched out a three-point sermon. When it came to teaching the kingdom, Jesus' methods were imperially simple. He either demonstrated his power—actually doing what he wanted people to see—or he captured their imaginations with subversive stories that got under their skin and forced them to chew on the truth a bite at a time. He used parables.

And that's why my idea would only work as a story. God wanted me to write a parable stuffed with unforgettably delectable images.

Very shortly after kicking myself—repeatedly—I scrapped eight years of work and started over. The story wrote itself in about two weeks. Honestly, I'm excited to see where it all leads, which is why I didn't invent some iconic 'Everyman' character you can relate to. It's about me, Brad Huebert. The protagonist is myself. In fact, many of the revelations I experience in the story represent real moments of profound struggle and triumph in my own life. I'm hoping that as I write, I'll keep changing—and that as you watch me change, you'll find yourself changing too.

My advice? Read this more than once, because there's a lot to chew on. I think this tale would lend itself well to a small group setting where you can flesh out what it might mean for day-to-day living together. And yes, this book is actually supposed to change the way you live your life. I believe it will do just that, if you let it.

One last thing: Since I'm the one writing the story, I'm going to take the liberty of indulging myself on one minor point: messing with my name and my family to make the story fit. Brad is a decent name, I suppose, but between you and me, I've always wanted a more epic title to hang my hat on.

So then: From this point onward, you will know me as … Ivan. Has a nice ring to it, don't you think? Sounds medieval. It's been said that people who view their life through an epic lens tend to find it more fulfilling. I totally agree, so that's where I'm going to take you. Or rather, that's where Ivan is going to take you.

The best thing about telling the truth with a story is that I can actually show you what I think Jesus means and gives and does without pages and pages of explanation. I can lead you by the hand and unveil the world as it might look if you could press through the clammy threshold of flesh to see with the eyes of faith. And maybe, just maybe, as we do that together, our eyes really will be opened and nothing will ever be the same for either of us.

Wouldn't that be amazing?

# Chapter One:
# Basileia

In the three hours since Monica had backed the silver minivan out of the driveway, Ivan had watched two mindless TV programs, wiped down the kitchen counter, eaten half an orange, mowed the back lawn, read four paragraphs of an article about migrating seals, opened the fridge to sniff the leftovers, and almost knelt down to hand over his life to Jesus at least a dozen times. He'd been what most people call a Christian for a long time, but the thought of total surrender just about gave him hives.

He glanced at the clock. Sixty-eight hours left of the weekend. Monica and Sarah had gone to Mom and Dad's to give him time to think, to get right with God. It seemed like a good idea at the time. Now they'd both gone, he missed them terribly, and he'd used up every distraction to pass the time he could think of. The time alone was probably a good thing, but the house was a whole lot warmer with his girls in it.

He picked up a framed photo of the three of them taken at the beach last summer. Ivan smiled wistfully. They were all standing by the old blue dock, arm in arm—but Monica and Sarah had something he didn't. Even the camera could see it. Their warmth. Their sparkle. He wanted it too— that simple faith, that joy—which meant he needed to hunker down, pray, and be done with it. No more excuses. It was time. Sliding off the couch, he dropped to his knees on the living room carpet, eyes clenched shut. No hives yet. He was determined not to move until the deed was done.

A giant sigh shuddered through him, finally releasing the prayer. It bubbled up like eager wine popping a stubborn cork. "I give up, Lord Jesus. And the answer is yes. I'm all yours."

As he spoke, the swirling fragments of his lukewarm faith found each other and took shape. Something shifted inside him. Died. Jumped to life. Laughed. All at once. His heart now belonged to the King of kings. He could feel it. Which meant he and his girls now shared another special bond. He had to call them.

Ivan opened his eyes, then scanned for the portable phone. The light around him had changed. And the air. A foreign breeze was snaking its way past him. A breeze?

Where was he?

He gasped. He was kneeling on a magnificent stone bridge—clean and white as snow glaring in the sun. It stretched more than a mile and he stood in the middle, right at the crest of its majestic arc. A cold rectangular spire thrust its way into the sky above him, and directly ahead the bridge sloped gently downward, eventually kissing a wall encircling a sparkling city on the mountain. The bridge spanned a throaty chasm. A bead of sweat snaked down from his hairline, stinging his eyes.

Where on earth was he?

Turning around, he saw another city parked at the other end of the bridge. But this one was inky black, dressed head-to-toe in a smothering dread and gloom. Toxic plumes of smoke billowed foul, as winged creatures circled like vultures above it. It looked as if the city were strewn with people waiting to die. The sight made his blood thicken.

The bridge between the cities was immovable but Ivan took tiny steps, moving tentatively toward the bright city. A gentle breeze held the place in a grave, empty silence. It felt not so much like a place as a place between places. The only real sounds came from his shuffling feet, his tongue smacking his lips, and his growling stomach.

The city looked like an ornate wedding cake baked onto a gold mountain. A thousand candy-green banners waved gently from the wall's ramparts and its towers were frosted by beautiful clouds. He also noticed with some relief that the front gate was wide open. It looked friendly enough. Again he wondered: Where was he?

As he neared the gate, hearty singing greeted him. The closer he came to the giant doorway, the louder the song became. That, and the city grew brighter. Was he dead? Was this the door into heaven? His heart leapt at the thought until he read the giant letters engraved above the gates:

*Basileia.*

Before he could ponder the name, people lit up with a prancing joy were streaming out of the gateway and cavorting toward him. Turning to look behind him to see who or what they were so excited to see, he saw nothing.

"You've come, you've come."

He whirled back around to meet a bent-over woman with a brown shawl. A dozen others with shining eyes and genuine smiles encircled him, hugging him and patting him on the back like he was some kind of war hero.

"Where am I?"

She raised her left eyebrow. "Why, you've come to Basileia, of course. You gave your heart to the King."

"Yes," Ivan replied, remembering his prayer. "But that happened in another place. Not here."

"Another place, yes," a little boy said, nodding in agreement. "From back there. From Kakos." He was pointing toward the black city. Ivan smiled at the boy, trying to help him understand.

"No, not from Kakos. I've never been there before."

"Yes, you have. We all have. We all come from the black city. We all come from Kakos."

Ivan was about to correct the child when the whole group said in unison, "Kakos is our mother, but Basileia is our home."

"Am I dead?"

"No, not dead," said the woman. "Alive, alive forevermore!"

"But is this heaven?" Ivan was growing impatient.

"We already told you," the first boy said, grinning. "It's Basileia! The kingdom of heaven!"

"But where is my family? My house? My car?"

The group laughed again, patting him on the back.

"We're your family now. Welcome here." With that, the whole crew turned around and frolicked their way back through the gate. Ivan blinked slowly, still befuddled.

Basileia? The kingdom? But not heaven itself? He didn't recognize any church friends in the group, and he was pretty sure he'd met all Monica's relatives. Who were these people? It was all too weird.

Slightly put off by the dancing greeters, he glanced back at the black city again and shuddered. He couldn't remember ever seeing Kakos before, but it did feel familiar. Even so, Ivan decided to take his chances inside Basileia. He marched himself through the giant gate.

Standing just inside, Ivan paused to get his bearings. A few paces ahead stood a wall—high, proud, and golden. To his left was an open archway, and to his right, an ascending stone staircase.

"Old City or New City?" asked a drawling voice to his left. He turned to see a portly man lobbing grins at him from his seat behind a merchant's cart. He was missing a few teeth and his tangled red hair flopped boorishly over his eyebrows. Ivan smiled in return.

"I'm new to Basila."

"Ba-sillay-uh," the man said slowly, cocking his head. His eyes popped wide suddenly. "Oh, I'm sorry. Ya don't even have yer book yet, do ya? I forgot."

"My book?"

"I'm supposed to give new people their book. That's my job." He grinned dumbly, holding out a thick leather-bound volume. "Here. Don't lose it, now."

Ivan took it and began flipping through the handsome pages. "What's it for?"

"Old City or New City?"

Ivan sighed, deciding he would get nowhere with the old cod. "Which do most people choose?"

"The Old City, most always." The man's face was expressionless.

"The Old City it is, then." Ivan strode toward the staircase.

"Then it tells ya how!" The man was trying to be helpful, but Ivan felt like he was being barked at by a simpleton.

"What?"

"The book. It tells ya how ta be a good citizen!"

"Great. Thanks." Ivan tucked the book under his arm, waving over his shoulder as he bounded up the steps. Time to figure out where he was.

Emerging on a cobblestoned second level, Ivan scanned his surroundings. He'd found some kind of ancient suburb or neighborhood. The city was slightly smaller here because it sat a little higher on the mountain. Dozens of townspeople were milling around him, minding their own business as they whistled through their tasks for the day. A bit farther down the street some kind of market sprawled toward him. At the urging of his complaining stomach, he decided to explore in that direction first. After a bite to eat, he would ask for directions.

The market was an earthy kaleidoscope of merchant's carts cascading with fresh produce, fish, strung chickens, and piles of colorful nuts.

"New to Basileia?"

Ivan turned to face one of the merchants, a middle-aged woman standing behind a pyramid of bright green apples.

"Yeah. I arrived just a few minutes ago."

"Well then, welcome home."

"Did you say, 'home'?"

"Here, try one." She tossed him an apple.

"Oh, I don't have any money."

"That's all right," she replied. Ivan bit hard into the fruit—partly because he was hungry and partly because he thought the rich sting of the apple might snap him back to his leather couch in the living room. It was a very good apple, but unfortunately his reality didn't budge. He was about to wander away to explore more of the city when he paused, rocking on his heels a moment.

"Something on your mind?" She raised a curious eyebrow.

"I've got this nagging sense that I ought to be doing something."

"Sure you do. We all have that. Some people think that once you arrive here the feeling will pass, but that's not true. It's usually a gentle pressure, kind of a weight put there by the King. If you're especially faithful the feeling actually grows. It's quite normal."

"Normal, huh? I'll take your word for it, but what should I do about the feeling for now?"

"Have you read your book yet? The book will tell you everything."

"I just got here. And to tell you the truth, I don't plan on staying. I need to get home."

"Well, if you read the book every day from now on, it will tell you what to do and answer your questions. See?" She pointed to the cover. Words had been sewn into the bleached leather, words Ivan was pretty sure hadn't been there when toothless Joe had held it out to him. The Book of Duties, apparently.

"Okay, it's like a Bible. Where do I start?"

The woman wiggled her way around the cart and strode over to him. Taking the book, she paged through it until she found a place near the beginning. She slipped a strip of brown paper between the pages and thumped the book closed. "There." She smiled as she returned the volume.

"Start slow. There is much to learn, and it can get pretty complicated later on. Just be sure not to miss temple on Tuesday."

"Temple?"

"All faithful citizens meet at the temple once a week to worship the King. The ceremony starts at eight in the evening."

"The King? You mean Jesus?"

"Yes. But here we just call him the King."

"Well, thank you for the apple and the advice. I guess I'll see you on Tuesday, if I haven't figured things out by then."

As he said the words, he noticed a quaint little park further up the street with a free bench in the shade. He decided to sit there for a while to read his new book. Maybe it would explain where he was and what he was supposed to do about it. If he were lucky, it would have a glossary at the back to help him understand all the new words he was hearing. Kakos. Basileia. Duty. Temple.

*Temple.* He called out to the woman again. One last question.

"Uh, what day is it today?"

"Monday."

"And that temple thing ..."

"On Tuesday. Tomorrow. Eight o'clock."

"Right."

# Chapter Two:
# The Book of Duties

As it turned out, Ivan did find a glossary of sorts near the back of the Book of Duties. Flipping through the pages, he soon discovered that Basileia meant "kingdom," and that Kakos meant "evil." Which made sense. He'd left his old life of failure and sin behind. He'd surrendered his whole heart to Jesus—or rather, the King. Apparently that meant living here in Basileia. Funny, his pastor had never mentioned that.

Even more important, where was Basileia? And how did he get here? He searched the index up and down, tracing it with his finger. Not a single entry that might explain how he got from his living room to this strange medieval kingdom. Truth be told, he might have thought twice about praying the prayer if he'd known what he was getting himself into. After all, what about his family? His friends back home? His job? His new car? Had he left all those things behind forever? Ivan shook his head. The King had changed everything he knew, everything he held dear. He had to get home as soon as possible. Maybe this was all a dream or some kind of bizarre vision. A virtual reality room for on fire Christians.

Finding the brown paper bookmark given to him by the merchant woman, he prayed again. "Lord—I mean, King—I'm not sure what's going on. I'm totally clueless here. I hope this book helps me get back home." He wondered if he would actually get to meet the King in person before leaving.

Ivan began reading. It didn't take long to see that the King had stacked a good chunk of the book with platitudinous lists. It was like his church back home, then. Being a free spirit, Ivan wasn't much of a list person, but if he was supposed to use the lists, use them he would. He felt like a clueless child having to learn how to live all over again. How to walk. How to talk. How to eat, how to conduct business, how to pray, how to worship. How on earth was he supposed to remember it all? Then he recalled the shrewd words of the merchant. "Take it slow. There is much to learn."

"I'll say." Ivan decided to choose one section for the time being and focus on putting that one into practice. Scanning the list of lists in the back of the book, he found one that said, "Devotional Correctness." He wasn't sure what "devotional" meant but he did know he wanted to be correct, so he flipped to page 381 and began to read.

"Good citizens of Basileia are devotionally correct citizens. Every good citizen must spend time every day reading the Book of Duties and praying to the King. It's what he expects of us. No exceptions."

It made sense, really. He'd given his heart to the King. No more fence-sitting. He would reserve the King a block of time every morning. That way once he found him, he'd have a few brownie points working in his favor. If the King was happy with him, maybe he would teleport him back into his living room or tell him to click his heels together or something like that. Ivan resolved to do whatever it took to please the King. There really was no place like home.

Reading on, Ivan found the following section very helpful. It outlined how much time to spend, how to develop that time, what to do during the time, and how to do it the way the King wanted. It was all so clear. He had a mission now. His heart pounded when he realized that at that very instant he was doing what the King had commanded him to do. Not only that, the birds were singing around him. The sun felt warm on his skin. No wonder people had been singing at the gate. Maybe he'd join them tomorrow. No, not tomorrow. He'd be gone by then, Lord willing.

Looking up from his reading, he got another surprise. Planted just across the cobbled street from the park sat a row of quaintly dressed houses. In the middle of the row was a newer looking unit, freshly painted, with a thick banner stretched across the front door. "Welcome home, Ivan," it read.

*Welcome home?* That had to be a mistake. Ivan leapt to his feet, almost forgetting his book on the bench. After scampering across the street, he bounced up the two steps to the door, ripped through the paper welcome, and grabbed the door handle, opening it with a creak.

"Hello?" His voice reverberated through the home, but no one answered. As he stepped into the entrance, he scanned the dwelling. The interior was simple but clean and attractive. A fresh cot had been made up in the corner, a fire was already busy in the stove, and a whimsically crooked window faced the outer wall of the city.

Still in shock, he padded up to the opening. It gave him a great view of the bridge, the chasm, and Kakos beyond it. Kakos. His mind reviewed all the things he'd learned in Sunday School growing up. Perhaps figuratively speaking he had come from the evil city, as the boy had insisted. And yet, Basileia wasn't figurative.

Just then Ivan spotted a crystal goblet perched on the kitchen table. A small note-card had been placed next to it. He picked up the ornate cup, snatching the note in his other hand. It was a personal message from the King.

"Ivan, have a drink on me. I hope to see you in the New City soon." It was signed, "the King."

Ivan's heart fluttered. A personal note from the King. Which meant he really could meet the King and find his way home. On the other hand, it would be fun to visit Basileia with his family once the confusion had been sorted out. As tourists, mind you. It was a fun place to visit, but not his first choice for a home.

The note gave Ivan a surge of energy. He sat at the table, savoring the freshly poured water in the goblet. He opened the book again, reading where he'd left off, poring over list after list after list, making notes and invoking the King's favor in hopes that he'd be able to keep all the commandments so he could learn to please him. The truth seemed overwhelming. Tipping the cup for another sip, he noticed to his chagrin that the water was gone. Too bad. It was the most refreshing water he'd ever tasted.

Pushing his chair back from the table, he decided to take a walk to pass the time and clear his head. The stroll through the park did him good, though he felt strangely weary in the late afternoon light. He noticed that the sun didn't seem as bright as it had when he arrived. Oddly enough, the buildings didn't seem so radiant either. He shook his head. Perhaps he was imagining it. After all, it had been a long, momentous day. Maybe he'd wake up at home the next morning. It was entirely possible that this whole adventure would turn out to be a vivid dream. Maybe his pastor could interpret it for him after church next week.

As he walked, he tried to remember what he'd learned in the Book of Duties. Every so often he saw something happening around him that reminded him of an entry on a list he had studied—a child in need, a woman requiring help. Most of the time he snapped into action, happily doing what the King expected of him in the situations that arose. It was like following the Bible.

But there was no end to it all. The needs were everywhere, and there was a command for everyone and everything. Sometimes two or three somethings sprung up at once and Ivan didn't know which command to obey. A few times he just froze, doing nothing. Frustration piled up in his heart. And then discouragement. He was too new at this. He wasn't Basileian enough yet. There was no way to obey every command on the giant list. Before long, he decided that enough was enough and called it a day. The sun was going down by then, so it seemed like the right thing to do—unless of course there was a rule against flagrant sulking. If there was, ignorance was his last shot at bliss.

Arriving at the house assigned to him exhausted and depressed, Ivan knelt beside his bed and muttered a long tearful prayer into the bedding, telling the King how very sorry he was for not keeping the list faithfully while secretly hoping he hadn't blown his opportunity to go home. He resolved to get up early the next morning to read more of the lists so he would stand a better chance at keeping them during the day. Somewhere in the middle of his prayer, still sprawled over the bed-frame, Ivan fell into a patchy sleep. He dreamt of Kakos, but strangely enough, it didn't seem like a nightmare. It felt like relief.

Ivan awoke to a deranged rooster crowing not far from his window. The creature's churlish call vibrated up and down his spine like an electric shock.

"I'm up, I'm up!" Ivan leapt from the bed, reacting as if he were required to report to the insipid bird. After stretching out some stiffness, his heart sank. He was still in Basileia. A moment later he remembered his promise to get up early to study and pray. Ivan rolled back onto his knees. They were tender from all the praying he had done the day before. He was just about to bow his head when he heard a knock at the door.

"What now?" Ivan stomped over to the door to answer. He swung it open and found the merchant woman standing on his porch. She cradled a basket of fresh green apples.

"Good morning." Her usual smile eclipsed her face again.

"Hello."

"Is this a bad time? I brought you more apples."

Ivan glanced back at the bed and his unopened Book of Duties. His eyes dropped to the floor. "No, it's fine. Come in."

"I see you're still here. How did you fare yesterday? Did you read the book?"

Ivan ushered her inside, then sat at the table as she set the basket on it. He rubbed his eyes. "I read some. Enough to keep me busy until bedtime yesterday."

Her eyes sparkled. "That's wonderful!"

"Wonderful? I failed miserably, and I'm exhausted."

"Well, it was your first day, after all."

"I guess." Ivan shifted in his seat.

"You're young in the faith, Ivan. You'll catch on." She did look convinced of that point.

Ivan didn't want to catch on. He wanted to go home. To have his life back. "What about you? You're mature in the faith. Do you keep the list perfectly?"

The woman paused, then bent in close, lowering her voice. She looked around pensively, as if to make sure no one was eavesdropping. "I'm going to tell you something." Her tone was flat. "We don't really talk about this, but the truth of the matter is that no one keeps the list perfectly."

"Really? No one?"

"That's right. But you eventually learn a few tricks to get around it."

"Tricks?"

"Well, not tricks, exactly. Call it a choice of emphasis. Did you notice that some things on the lists are more public and obvious, while others are more inward and hidden?"

"Yes, I suppose so, but aren't …"

She didn't let him finish. "Focus on the public ones, Ivan. The ones that people see. Then they'll assume the other rules they can't see are being kept too."

Ivan was confused. "If you're all faking it, don't you know that beneath the surface other people are mixed up just like you are? No offense."

"None taken. It's a mutual understanding we extend to each other. And we don't talk about it, not even with newcomers. At least, not usually."

"Well, thanks," Ivan said, vaguely appreciative. But something felt off. True, he wanted to get home to see his family, but if the King was real, he had to honor his prayer to him. He had surrendered his life to Christ. "What other people think is just half of it. It's what I feel when I fail that hurts the most. I can't stand letting the King down after all he's done for me."

"But that's the beauty of it. Focusing on the outward rules creates a kind of mask you can hide behind. Even when you look in the mirror. And you're doing the public things. That means you're checking off about half the list, right?"

"I guess. Does it work for you?"

"Mostly." She shrugged her shoulders dispassionately. "Here, I'll show you."

To Ivan's astonishment, she peeled off her face. No, not her face. A mask that looked like her face with a plastic smile splitting it. Her real face was scored by onerous wrinkles of disappointment and sadness. Apparently embarrassed to be seen without her mask, she quickly slipped it back on. In a few moments she had stretched it back across her face and he couldn't tell she was wearing it. "There! See? That's better."

And actually, she did look better with the mask on. "But the King knows, doesn't he? How can you experience all the King's blessings if you can't be good enough to earn them? Isn't that what life here is all about?"

"To experience the King's gifts and blessings, you must ask him. No one ever received without asking. And before you ask, you must please him. And while you ask him, you must have faith. Faith comes with a saintly stubbornness. He wants you to press him. You must find his promises in the book among the lists, and claim them for yourself."

"Claim them?"

"Write them down. Memorize them. Bring them up every time you talk to the King. Remind him to keep his promises, and persevere in your asking until he gives you what you ask for."

"He wants us to bother him?" Ivan felt confused. "If he's real and he's here, why doesn't he just give us what we need?"

"He does, he does. But it usually takes some desperation. Some work. If you haven't received what you want, it's because you haven't asked passionately enough. Or because you need more devotional correctness. Or there may be sin in your life. You'll see."

Ivan felt dejected. It all sounded so complicated. His chair suddenly felt uncomfortable.

"No, no—there's no sense fighting it, Ivan. That's how the King has designed his kingdom. It's the law."

"The law, huh? Well, if you say so. But does it actually work?"

"Not always." She shrugged her shoulders again. "Blessings come, blessings go. I guess you just kind of have to lower your expectations."

"That's not exactly why I surrendered to the King." Her words caused a churchly discouragement to gnaw at his soul. For now, he was almost able to push it aside, even without a mask to help him. But he missed his girls terribly.

# Chapter Three:
# The Pursuit

After his visitor left, Ivan read a few more lists and then slammed the book shut, trying to muzzle his guilt. He felt like even walking out the door doomed him to failure, but then realized that staying put was letting the King down too. He opted for the indoor kind of failure because he wasn't ready to don one of those masks just yet, and failing in front of people felt worse somehow. He almost stayed home from temple too, harrowed with shame as he was—but he had to do one thing right and the woman had mentioned that every good citizen of Basileia went to temple. Plus, it was a public thing that people would notice. Her punctilious excuses were beginning to work their magic on him.

Ivan's spirits lifted some as he left his dwelling at 7 p.m., which he hoped was early enough to get a good seat. Apparently the giant building was parked on the back side of the mountain, which conveniently put it just out of sight of the bridge, the chasm, and particularly the gloomy city of Kakos. They'd chosen a great location—no sense thinking about all those dying people all evening. It made for a longer walk, but he needed the fresh air since he had opted to stay inside all day.

Slowly orbiting the mountain along the perimeter road, Ivan noticed more and more people joining him on the walk. He also noticed the rooftops of the buildings on the level below, the so-called "new" city, and pondered what life might be like for people down there. Probably a lot like life where he was. He would have to ask his new friend about that.

He arrived at the temple just as the sun was giving up on the day, so he was glad for the lamplight inside. The building was a grandiose monolith built to inspire awe. He was greeted at the door by friendly citizens who shook his hand heartily as he came in the door. He almost felt at home—almost—until he remembered his friend's unguarded disclosure. They were all modeling disguises, meaning he'd better play the part too. With considerable effort, he began to smile broadly. In the end it wasn't so bad. With every step his face stiffened a little but his outlook brightened a few shades to compensate.

Ivan had never seen such a big auditorium, but his real joy was that he would finally see the King for himself. A large stone podium waited at the front of the cavernous room where the King would apparently stand to address them. As early as Ivan was, he was still only able to find a seat halfway to the back. It wasn't the best seat in the house, but it gave him a decent view. Looking up, his jaw went slack in awe. The auditorium had several levels, each with its own posh seating. He saw at least two more levels above him.

"I should probably get as high up as I can," he thought, leaving his seat for the upper levels. But after ten minutes of searching, it became obvious that there were no stairways from his level to the ones above. Rushing back to the auditorium, Ivan found himself sitting in one of the last remaining seats in the back. He chided himself for giving up his first seat.

As eight o'clock drew nearer, the buzz of temple conversations trailed off into a pious silence as a man dressed in a black robe paraded his way to the podium. Was this the King? The object of his heart's desire? Ivan hoped not.

"Thank you all for coming. Bow your heads, and let us pray."

Ivan didn't bow his head. The man obviously wasn't the King, and he didn't want to miss the moment when the real King took the stage. But the King didn't come. The man prayed and prayed—and prayed—vociferously, at that—and still no King. Near the end of the prayer, the man said, "Oh gracious King, we ask in your benevolent name that you would grace us with your presence today. Come, O King, and dwell among us. Come. We have left everything at the door—everything we have done, everything on our minds, everything that matters to us, and have come before you with empty hearts waiting for your breath to fill us."

Ivan looked around. Still no King. But many of the people had raised their hands, stretching them out high into the air like naked tree branches in winter. It looked to Ivan like they were begging for something. *Come, O King*, the man had prayed. Did that mean the King was somewhere else? That perhaps he wouldn't come at all and had to be asked? What if they hadn't asked him properly? Or fervidly enough? What if he was busy or out of the country? Ivan's heart slumped low and stayed there all the way through several songs that he didn't know, full of words he would have to look up later in the glossary of his new book. The melodies were beautiful, but they chimed hollow because they were about joy and peace and all kinds of things he didn't feel right then.

"Sing, sing your hearts out to the King," the song leader shouted. "The harder we sing, the more we will feel his presence. Come, O King, and dwell in our praises." Ivan wondered how many people actually felt the King, because he couldn't tell through their masks. But if singing enthusiastically regardless of how he was feeling was part of being a good citizen, so be it. Ivan sang along.

Soon afterward, the man in black took the podium for a second time and began to speak. He opened an impressive copy of the Book of Duties—which was much larger than Ivan's copy—and began to read. He dictated an inspiring story about the King, which made Ivan pay closer attention. Finally, the story ended and the man looked up.

"We must all seek the King for ourselves." He closed the book with a holy thump. "If we seek him, we will find him."

"We must all seek the King for ourselves," the crowd said in unison, but Ivan missed the moment and was the only one still repeating the words when the crowd fell silent. He blushed, and with that, the holy man was praying again.

"We thank you, O King, for being here with us today. Help us to be faithful citizens. Go with us now. In your name, amen."

Amen? But the King hadn't come at all. Ivan was confused. Was temple a kind of mask too?

"Seek, seek, seek …" the crowd said together. With that, they got up from their seats and dispersed into the night. Ivan shook his head, but still found himself curious about seeking the King. There was something to that, he decided. Perhaps it would help him keep the list, which would rack up the brownie points he needed to ask the King for his ticket home.

Ivan awoke to the kitschy rooster again, slightly less startled than the first morning but noticeably more annoyed with the infernal creature. Ivan realized once again that he'd slept in—apparently roosters in Basileia rose later than in other places. It was the bird's fault.

A moment later he cursed himself for missing his early morning appointment with the Book of Duties. Not a good start to the day. Snatching another apple, he held it with his teeth while tying the belt on his tunic, telling himself that he would get to his reading later on. Pushing his guilt aside, he decided to wear his new mask—for a day or two, tops—while he found his stride in Basileia. It was only temporary. When in Rome, do as the Romans do. His first priority was to find his merchant friend and ask her about that King-seeking business.

Meandering past the park and down the street toward the riotous market, Ivan noticed that a wall of featureless clouds had painted the city in a mackerel gray. The resplendent colors he'd seen on his first day had been replaced by a whey-faced palette. He reasoned that he must have been seeing the city through a naive optimism at first.

"Good morning." He beamed at his new friend when she looked up.

"Why, good morning." She winked at him. "I see you've found a mask to your liking. It suits you."

"Thank you, thank you." Ivan dipped in a mock bow. "But I don't plan on wearing it for very long. I'm here to talk to you about seeking the King. I think that's what I've been missing since I arrived here."

"Ah, right you are, but I'm not the one you need to talk to. Visit old Simeon down the road. He lives in the steep-roofed home and has been seeking the King longer than any of us. If you want to properly begin the Pursuit, he's the one you should see."

"The Pursuit, huh? All right. I'll go see him."

"Nomothesia," she said.

"What?"

"That's my name. Nomothesia."

Ivan smiled. "Then thank you, Nomothesia." He would have to look that word up in the back of the book.

"You've been enjoying the apples I left you, haven't you?" She was teasing him.

Ivan tipped his head. "Why, yes, I have. How did you know?"

"Your thirst for knowledge. That's what the fruit does. Which is good. the more we know, the more of the King's blessing we can enjoy."

It seemed true enough. The apples invigorated him, giving him a thirst for knowledge when he was discouraged. "Well, then, thanks again and keep the apples coming."

"I will, I will."

Leaving the market behind, Ivan sauntered into the suburb he'd seen on his first day in Basileia. Sure enough, one of the homes stood out from all the others with a roof pitched so steeply that it looked like a rocket aimed at the heavens. The house of a true seeker. His ticket home.

He was about to knock on the front door when he noticed a note tacked to the wood.

"Out chasing down a sighting of the King in the park. I may be awhile." It was signed, "Simeon."

A sighting of the King? In the park? Ivan charged back down the cobbled road as fast as his legs could take him. He passed a few other citizens also scampering in that direction. Perhaps they'd caught a whiff of the rumor as well. He barreled back through the market and bumbled his way into a simple clearing in the park. A man was kneeling there, arms outstretched to the sky. Old man Simeon, apparently. But no King.

But he was still making progress. Ivan was so excited to find Simeon that he barged right over to him, breathless and impatient. His words came out in bursts.

"I'm Ivan … Nomothesia sent me … I want to find the King!"

"Oh, you just missed him." Simeon spoke cheerfully, though Ivan caught a smidgen of sadness lingering in the man's voice.

"You *saw* him?"

"Well, not exactly." Simeon lowered his arms and turned to face him. "But he was here. Look! His footprints are right there in the dirt."

Ivan inspected the earth at Simeon's feet. An indistinct something had depressed some dirt in a few places but it was hard to make out. Ivan never would have noticed the tracks if Simeon hadn't highlighted them.

"I want you to teach me to seek the King. I want to see what you see."

"Ahhh, the great Pursuit," Simeon rubbed his hands together gleefully. "Walk with me and I will instruct you." The old man extended his hand to Ivan, and he heaved Simeon to his feet.

"The King loves us, and we must love him in return," the sage explained as they strolled along. "We can't see him, but we must seek him nonetheless. He could be right with us now, in fact—invisible to our eyes."

"I think I understand. When the man in the black robe at the temple was praying, I heard him asking the King to come into the service."

"Yes, that is a common prayer. The King reigns high above us, so we must invite him to come down to be a part of our everyday lives."

"What if we forget to ask him? What if we don't seek him like we should?"

"Then I'm afraid we're on our own."

Ivan nodded, then stopped. "But if you can't see him, how do you know if he's come?"

"He leaves his footprints and fingerprints for us to chance upon. Sometimes we recognize his whisper in the breeze, or catch a whiff of his sacred fragrance on the wind. And every so often—though you mustn't get your hopes up—he leaves us a note on the kitchen table to read."

Ivan gasped. "He left me a note on the table the day I arrived."

"You see? The trick is to live for those moments, longing for the days when he appears to us, waiting for him to come down from above and touch our lives. The most noble citizens of Basileia are the most passionate seekers. And he rewards passion that is proven."

"I feel that passion right now," Ivan said, breathless.

"I can see it on your face. You must put everything else in second place to that passion. You must seek the King with all your heart. If you seek him with all your heart, you will find him. Then and only then."

"Have *you* found him?" The question seemed to rock old Simeon.

"Well … no. But I'm getting closer every day. You see, that's the secret. We all begin far away from the King. Keeping the list faithfully and seeking him, praying to him and reading the Book of Duties—all of these move us closer to him. Breaking the rules and not seeking the King pushes us away. He waits for faithful citizens to draw near, to pay the price for true intimacy with him."

"I want … I *need* to pay the price." Ivan felt an adrenalized fire surging in his heart.

"I know you will." Simeon patted him on the shoulder. "But I must be off. Sometimes the King has been spotted at the southern well. It is my custom to go there in the afternoons just in case he passes by."

"Maybe I'll join you later. First I need to go home and study my Book of Duties."

"A wise choice. Make sure to memorize the verses. That pleases the King very much. You won't find him if he's not pleased with you."

And with that, Ivan left Simeon to his Pursuit and marched off toward his temporary home. His stomach growled for another one of Nomothesia's apples.

Enflamed by Simeon's challenge, Ivan spent the rest of the week fully engaged in the Pursuit. Every waking moment he thought about the King—asking him to come, foraging for clues, calling out his name, rushing off to places where the King had recently been. He pored over the Book of Duties every morning for half an hour, memorizing the parts that seemed important for proving his peerless devotion. In the process he found several commanding truths he was certain would help him chance upon the King. Even so, by the end of each day he still felt like he was one critical insight away from discovering the master principle that would clear up the mystery and guarantee his heart's desire. Unfortunately, every silver bullet seemed to misfire, leaving him no closer to finding his way home than the day he'd arrived.

Every day from dawn till way past bedtime Ivan tried his best to comply with all the instructions on the lists. He spent protracted hours memorizing the King's promises and transcribing them to bits of parchment. He waved them in the air as he prayed, reminding the King of his promises and claiming those blessings for himself. It was stodgy work, but he was certain that he was becoming a better citizen. Certainly better than many of the people living around him. That had to count for something.

Every once in a while Ivan would catch a whiff of the King's scent on the night air or find a partial footprint gracing the soft earth. A couple of times he even found a short note from the King on his kitchen table. Ivan longed to go home, but meeting the King would be amazing in and of itself.

Before long, Ivan began to live for those fleeting moments when the King seemed to be near. It was as if the King was saying, "Keep looking. You're getting warmer." The King never used those words, of course, but how could he miss the message? Unfortunately, most of the time the King did not seem nearer or warmer. In fact, most of the time it felt as if he were on some cosmic business errand infinite universes away, which left Ivan feeling cold and empty. The sporadic notes and hints vitalized him at first, but after a while it felt like the King was teasing him or playing hard to get. Near the end of the week he felt he was playing a giant game of cat and mouse—as though the King were dangling fresh clues just out of reach with no intention of letting Ivan catch them. Hide and seek was a fun game to play but a terrible way to live.

Even worse, word got out that a few people in his neighborhood had spent time with the King face to face that week. One family even hosted him for a late supper, then vanished along with him. What were they doing for the King that he wasn't? In the end he couldn't think of a single thing to do differently besides reading more of the Book of Duties and praying harder and longer.

So he did. But no matter how much progress he made in his devotional correctness, the King was nowhere to be found. Soon his frustration had frothed itself into a bubbling anger—all hidden behind his smiling mask, of course. The mask had become a daily necessity by this time. He felt exposed and naked without the rubbery thing, only taking it off in the seclusion of his own home. He yearned to talk to Monica, wondering if he would ever see her or his precious Sarah again. He ached to go home, for life to return to normal.

How was he supposed to follow someone he couldn't see, hear, touch, feel, or find? If the King never showed up, how was that any different than being stood up? And how could he build a relationship with someone who was only around when he didn't notice? Any hopes Ivan had entertained of befriending the King or going home had been stretched so ridiculously thin by now that they felt they might snap at any moment. Why would the King hide himself like this? Why would he withhold the key to his heart if he wanted to have a relationship with his subjects?

Rumor had it that the King lived at the top of the Mountain. That had to be it. With his desperation deepening, Ivan sold his home and found a new one up on the Third Level—one step closer to the peak hidden by the clouds. He hoped this sort of bold move would count for something. In theory it would move him closer to the King and signal his unmatched devotion. Higher and harder, that was his motto. But by the end of the second day in his new place the excitement of the move had evaporated and his new location didn't seem to matter. Still no King. It wasn't fair. He was more than paying the price for intimacy, but the King seemed oblivious to his dedication.

Fair or not, Ivan couldn't ignore the vapid pang ravishing his hope. He often dreamt about drawing closer to the King and ached to connect with him soul to soul. By now his heart felt like a withering desert plant, and in weaker moments he thought of giving up the Pursuit altogether. He was a failure at seeking the King and keeping his lists. He was a pitiful citizen. How would he ever get home if he couldn't make the cut? Tears burned his eyes as he thought of Monica and Sarah wondering where he'd gone. As discouraged as he was, he would not, he could not, give up.

He surmised that he must still be missing something important. But what?

# Chapter Four:
# The Spring of Thirst

The following Tuesday Ivan left the temple with a smothering heaviness blanketing his heart. He made no effort to get anything meaningful out of the service. What did it matter? He was stuck in life, stuck in this stupid place. As he exited the auditorium, he spied Simeon among the supplicants.

"Simeon." Ivan felt desperation rising like a lump in his throat. The man turned and gaped at him blankly. "It's me. Ivan." Simeon's eyes flickered in partial recognition. Apparently he was so consumed with pursuing the King that everyone else had faded from view.

"Yes, I remember you. How are you faring with the Pursuit?"

Ivan sighed, not caring whether the man remembered him or not. "Not very well. I catch fleeting glimpses of the King, but mostly I see nothing, hear nothing, and feel nothing."

"Do you feel empty inside?"

"Every single day."

"Marvelous. That's something." Simeon's eyes were gleaming.

"Marvelous?"

"Yes, yes. It means your heart belongs to the King. Without thirsting for him, without hungering deeply for his fellowship, you will never find him. You are getting closer, my young pupil."

"I am?"

"Absolutely. The most spiritual citizens in Basileia are the ones with the most ravaging thirst for the King. If we thirst for him, we will be satisfied by him."

Ivan's mind began putting the pieces together. The city was a living illustration of faith. "So keeping the list and studying the Book of Duties every day is like the Second Level of Basileia."

"Yes! And those who commit to the Pursuit ascend to the Third Level. Which is why, without even knowing why, you moved up to live in the Third Level of the city."

Ivan's heart pounded in his chest. "That's right. I did move up here, didn't I? So I'm on the right track?"

"Yes. But now you must sell your home and move to the Fourth Level."

"What? I just got here." Ivan's heart sank.

"Do you want to keep ascending the ladder of the King's graces? Do you still want to pay the price, no matter what the cost? The Book of Duties does say, "You shall love the King with all your heart, with all your mind, and with all your strength.""

"I read that yesterday." Ivan felt strength and hope burgeoning within him again.

"Come, come," Simeon said. "I'll show you to the Fourth Level."

"But my things …"

"You can get them later."

Ivan nodded, following the doddering old man through the city streets until they reached another staircase, narrower than the first two and much steeper. Ivan was sure that Simeon would be unable to ascend the stairs, but after a few dozen gasps and lurches they had spilled over onto the Fourth Level.

"I used to … live here." Simeon put his hands on his hips, trying to catch his breath. "But as you can see, my legs … and lungs … aren't what they used to be."

"The Fourth Level sure is smaller than the Third."

"And the Fifth is smaller still. The path narrows as we near the King, and fewer live at each level because fewer citizens are willing to sell all to have the pearl."

"The pearl?"

"Look it up in the book. Come, follow me."

Simeon led Ivan along the ring road, and before long they had found a whimsical neighborhood a little smaller than the one he had left behind and far more modest. Nothing was dressed up or refined like in the Second and Third Levels. Ivan guessed those living on the Fourth Level were so passionate about the King that such frivolities no longer wooed them. It didn't take the pair long to locate Ivan's new dwelling, a fresh two-bedroom apartment overlooking the lower levels, the bridge, the chasm, and the city of Kakos sulking in the distance. It had been awhile since he had thought about the dark city. "When I arrived, the welcoming party said that we all come from Kakos."

Simeon joined him at the window. He stood there for a full minute before responding. "They were speaking the truth."

"How did I ... I mean, how do people ..."

"How is it that people living in Kakos come to live in Basileia? They must give their heart to the King. You know that."

"But how are they supposed to find out about the King?"

"We must tell them. We have to reach out to them."

"But since I've been here, no one has talked much about that. Should we be crossing the bridge over into Kakos to talk to their citizens?"

"Heavens, no." Simeon shuddered. "Foolish renegades from the New City often go there, but no one in the Old City would even dream of such a thing. If Kakosians want to come to Basileia, they can come to us. We send them invitations to attend temple every week, but they rarely choose to come. Their loss."

Ivan barely heard Simeon's last sentence. "What about the New City?"

"The New City is for dreaming simpletons. Did you know that the entire New City sits on the lower level of Basileia, set below our very First Level? Think how far they live from the peak. Think about how much closer to the King you are."

"It was brighter down there." Ivan felt his face stiffen with sadness.

"That's because we are ascending into the clouds, Ivan."

"Maybe they aren't clouds, Simeon. Maybe it's a fog. I had forgotten until now, but in his first note, the King said something about meeting him in the New City."

Simeon sighed. "A common misunderstanding. Come with me, young one. You have much to learn." Simeon grabbed Ivan's sleeve and then led him away from the window. Both Ivan and Simeon gasped as they passed through the kitchen. There was another note centered on the tabletop leaning against a crystal goblet full of sparkling water. The sight made Ivan's heart sing.

27

"Ivan, I miss you. Please enjoy this drink, on me. It will refresh your spirit. When are you coming to the New City? I'm waiting for you there." It was signed by the King.

"Ha. You see? He misses me." Ivan waved the note in Simeon's face. "And he mentioned the New City. He wants me to visit him there."

Simeon's countenance darkened. He shook his head slowly. "It's a trick."

"A trick?"

The old man strode over to the window. He pulled the shades to cover the opening. "Come to temple on Tuesday and you will see."

"But the King ..."

"Trust me. Do nothing rash until you hear the preacher. He will help you understand. And whatever you do, don't even think of drinking this water."

Ivan was confused. "Why not?"

"If the note is a fake, the drink may well be poisoned. Think, Ivan. Why would the King give you a goblet of his royal water when you're living on the Fourth Level, the very place where his Spring of Thirst flows free for all to drink?"

"I don't know. Maybe ..."

"Perhaps I should get you to the well. One sip of that water will show you the truth."

Ivan let his shoulders slump. He had honestly believed the note was genuine. "So the note isn't really from the King?"

"I'm afraid not." Simeon patted him on the shoulder. "The enemy counterfeits the King's gifts all the time. Most miracles are counterfeits."

Ivan felt too dejected to argue. "Well, then, I suppose you should just take me to the well." He didn't have to wait long. The seven-tiered fountain sat not five minutes from his apartment. Majestic pillars flanked the central pool, which was now surrounded by a hundred people excitedly drawing water into cups, urns, buckets, and even flagons.

"Behold the Spring of Thirst." Simeon grinned, waving his arms theatrically.

"It's beautiful," Ivan said, just as much to himself as to Simeon.

"Drink, drink."

"May I? I mean, is it free?"

"Of course it's free. Haven't you read? We may come and drink and have our fill at no cost."

"I guess I haven't gotten that far yet. " Ivan stepped carefully toward the sensational pool, while Simeon shoved his way through thirsty pilgrims until he had found the edge. He bent over the railing suddenly, tipping himself forward until his feet left the ground and his lips met the surface. He drank deeply and his body shuddered with apparent delight. Rocking himself back up to a standing position, he wiped his mouth with his sleeve, grinning from ear to ear. "Drink, Ivan. Drink."

Ivan needed no further encouragement. Bending over as his new mentor had, he leaned in close until he could test a tiny sip's worth. It was delicious.

"What do you think?" Simeon clapped his hands in childlike delight. "Well?"

Ivan had to think for a moment. Then another. "It tastes like … like …"

"Yes?"

"It tastes like more." Ivan plunged his entire face into the pool, drinking as fast as he could take it in without choking.



Over the next few days Ivan found himself returning often to the fountain for refills of the King's water. By the end of the week he could hardly go two hours without the stuff. Between Nomothesia's magic apples and the Spring of Thirst he could barely contain his swelling passion for fellowship with the King. And the thirst produced a welcome side effect—he never missed his daily appointment with the Book of Duties. His appetite for the lists grew parallel with his thirst, and his devotional correctness became more consistent. He fasted one meal a day, engaged in retreats of silence, and even memorized large portions of the book. He was on his way to pleasing the King and earning his ticket home.

True, he didn't see or hear the King at all, but he was sure his devotion would pay off sooner or later. Ivan resolved that when the King came calling, he would find him both thirsty and faithful. The only drawback was that he had lost some weight and felt weaker than he had in a long time. But no matter. If his fasting and prayer pleased the King, then fast and pray he would. His family was worth it.

The night before temple, Ivan reclined in his new bed, relishing the joy filling his heart. Who would have thought that thirsting for the King would be the key to growth in his kingdom? True, the King had promised that all who came to him would be satisfied, but Ivan now saw that the promise was about the bliss between drinks, not satisfaction as a way of life.

Ivan could hardly wait for the upcoming temple gathering. Trying to quiet himself, he finally gave up on sleeping. He tiptoed out the front door to make his way back to the pool for another drink, trying not to disturb his neighbors. To his surprise, at least twenty people were already there, every one turning to grin at him sheepishly under the full moon.

"Thirsty, huh?" A young boy stood before him.

Ivan wondered where the lad's parents were. "You bet. That's why I'm here."

A teenage girl was also enjoying the pool. She wasn't shy either. "It's amazing, isn't it? The more you drink, the more you need. The more you want the King. I feel like I'd die without this way of life."

"I've been coming here for ten years and I still can't get enough," a middle-aged man said, joining the conversation. "It satisfies you and intensifies your thirst at the same time."

Ivan looked over at the man and smiled, but when he saw him his smile evaporated. "Are you okay?"

"Me? Sure. I'm just thirsty. Thirsty for the King."

But the man didn't look thirsty. He looked deathly sick. Deep hollows hung around his vapid eyes.

"Just out of curiosity, when was the last time you saw the King?" he asked the man.

"Personally? Not for years."

"Not for years?" Ivan was shocked. "And you're proud of it? I thought thirsting for the King would please him. That he would reveal himself to us more often."

"Then you've misunderstood."

"But I have to get home." Ivan felt faint. "I need my family. I …"

"Home? This is home. Get used to it."

"But I thought … I thought …"

"How do you make someone thirsty, son? By satisfying them? No, by depriving them. By starving them. By keeping water from them."

"But he's given us the spring," Ivan said.

"To make us thirsty. This isn't really water, you know. Real water would quench our thirst." The man looked insane in the otherworldly moonlight. His eyes were wild, bulging from his gaunt frame.

Ivan's heart pounded. "What?"

"It's true! Water would quench our thirst. But then we wouldn't thirst for the King, would we? And what would be the good of that? You're more spiritual now than you've ever been." The man's voice grew louder as he spoke. "Take a good look at yourself, friend. You're a gaping hole."

Glancing down at his reflection in the pool, Ivan gasped. It was true. He saw a ghost, a walking skeleton. It was then that he noticed his lips. They were cracked and swollen. His arms were cadaverous and weak. His scalp smoldered with fear. What was wrong with him? Stumbling back from the fountain, he lost his balance and then flopped onto his backside.

Ivan's breathing became more rapid and shallow. Stars began to dance before his eyes. He had to get back to his apartment, to calm down, to rest. Pushing himself to his feet, he forced himself to move. All he could manage was a tottering, dizzy gait across the uneven stones. It was stubborn fear alone that managed to drive him back to his dwelling without fainting. The moment he stepped inside, his legs gave up and he sprawled onto all fours. Staring at the tan tiles and gasping for breath, Ivan tried to command his withered muscles. It was only with the greatest effort that he was able to wrangle his feverish body onto his cot. Shivering there in the dark, he tried to pray.

"King, I don't understand. I'm thirsty for you, just like you wanted. I'm reading my book faithfully. I'm learning to keep the lists. I'm seeking you all day long and fasting and praying. I'm going to temple every week. I just want to go home."

Breaking down completely, Ivan began to sob. "Help me, King. Please." It was then that he remembered the bogus note and the goblet on the kitchen table. Simeon had insisted it was a fake, that the liquid in the cup was poison. But Ivan didn't care. If it was poison then he would drink to his misery, and this nightmarish religion would finally come to an end and he would wake up in bed at home.

After rolling himself off the bed, he heaved his stiffening body across the cold floor, eventually reaching the kitchen. Pulling together a last reservoir of strength, he propped himself up and paused to catch his breath. The goblet was still there on the table. Snagging the cup with the tips of his trembling fingers, he slid it slowly toward himself, then brought it to his lips. Time to end the journey. He downed the whole thing in a few clumsy gulps. A few seconds later he felt his mind slipping away. He embraced the blackness.

# Chapter Five: Battle

Ivan awoke at suppertime the following day, perplexed at how refreshed and content he felt. He lay there on the floor for a long time, both getting his bearings and wondering if the episode at the fountain the night before had only been a nightmare. His skin crawled as he remembered his conversation with the sickly middle-aged man, his dreadful reflection in the water, and the frantic journey back to the apartment. It was then that he noticed that his front door had been left wide open. He also saw the King's goblet lying on its side beside him on the floor. The nightmare had apparently been quite real.

But he was also alive and somehow at peace. The King's water? That had to be it. Holding up his hand to his face, he was dumbfounded at the sight. His fingers were pink, his palm was meaty, and his arm was no longer skeletal. Touching his face, he tried to trace the contour of the deep hollows he had found there the night before and felt only a full, blushing cheek filling his hand.

Ivan began to cry. Slapping the tiles euphorically, he also began to laugh. The joy came so hard that his sides hurt, so fast that he couldn't breathe. It wasn't long before tears glazed his face and he wasn't sure whether he was laughing, crying, or both. When the outburst had run its course, he looked up at the ceiling, smiling.

"Thank you, King. That was a wonderful gift. I'm going to go down to the New City today. I just have to ..."

His prayer was interrupted by a bawdy trumpet blast that made him jump. A moment later it sounded again. Soon he could hear people running through the streets. A loud *pom pom pom* sound joined the mayhem. Someone was clobbering a drum so hard that his heart jumped at the cadence. What was going on? After bouncing to his feet, he stumbled to the open doorway just as a muscle-bound soldier was marching by. Spying Ivan, he stopped to address him.

"Don't stand there looking dumb as your doorpost. Where's your armor, soldier?" Spittle sprayed as he spoke.

"You must be mistaken. I'm not a soldier." Ivan found himself retreating a step or two into his apartment.

"What?" The man's veins were bulging like angry balloons from his neck. "Every citizen of Basileia is a soldier. Every citizen must fight. And we're at war, in case you hadn't heard."

Ivan felt the blood drain from his newly blushed cheeks. War? He couldn't believe it. "Isn't this a peaceful kingdom? I don't …"

With that, the impatient soldier stomped up to him, grabbed him by the scruff of his neck, and hauled him like a rebellious child into the middle of the street. The strong arms spun him around to face the direction of Kakos. "There! Look for yourself."

Ivan did look. He saw the giant cloud hanging over mournful Kakos as usual. This morning the haze was moving, advancing toward them, drawing nearer every moment. But it wasn't a haze. It was an army, a thousand winged creatures of pooling blackness flapping toward Basileia in battle formation. The Old City's collective dread was palpable.

"Unless you want to get eaten alive, I suggest you haul yourself to the temple and slap your armor on," the soldier said, letting Ivan go. "And take up your sword. I expect to see you on the front lines. Got it?"

Ivan nodded, mesmerized by the advancing maelstrom. A sword? He'd never been at war before—or held a sword, or shot a bow, or anything like that. This wasn't a video game. He had to get himself to the temple.

After scrambling back and forth frantically for ten minutes Ivan realized there was no entrance into the temple from Level Four. He decided to brave his way up to the Fifth Level. The path had been chiseled out from a cliff wall and climbed more like a ladder than a stairway. Once he reached the Fifth Level, Ivan took a moment to get his bearings. The Fifth Level was the smallest of all, housing less than half of the population scrunched into the level he'd come from. Every citizen he saw was either decked out in full armor or marching toward the temple—apparently to get outfitted. He joined the marchers and within a few minutes found himself standing in a lineup of grim Basileians waiting for their gear. A tall man stood behind the desk, wiping stray droplets of sweat from his eyes.

Ivan noticed piles of armor covering the greasy counter—one for helmets, one for swords, and a few more—breastplates, girdles, and boots. He picked up a dented helmet from its pile. "How much?"

"It's free, compliments of the King."

"So …"

"One of each, and please keep moving."

"Which?"

"One size fits *all*, sir." The man was clearly growing impatient, drawing out his syllables to sound condescending. Not wanting to cause a scene, Ivan loaded his arms full of armor and perched the sword on top. The stuff was heavy. He wondered if he would be able to move once he'd put it on. Ivan felt awkward and confused. What was he supposed to do? He found a regal knight already outfitted for battle and worked up the courage to ask the warrior a question.

"Did I miss the sermon today? I didn't even see a place for seating in there."

"Seating?" The man laughed a tin laugh behind his visor. "This is battle level, boy. Kill or be killed. Learn as you go. Moses had time for prayer, but Joshua was a man of steel. If I were you, I'd get that armor on pretty quick. And do it every day without fail. The diabolon are upon us." The soldier gripped his sword and lunged for cover under a rooftop. Seconds later the breeze vibrated with howls and roars that would have been heard from miles away. But they were closer than that. Much closer. The air crackled with dark power.

The soldier was shouting now. "Run, man. And keep your shield up."

A moment later a cold shadow snaked across the ground in front of him. A coal-black lion with a snow-white mane and cruel reptilian wings was circling the rooftops above them. Ivan found himself stunned into silence. Then two diabolon were circling. Then three. After dropping his helmet in clumsy fear, Ivan turned and bolted for a nearby alleyway, holding his bundle of armor just as the roaring creature streamed past. The knight across the street was bellowing at him again. "Your helmet, you fool. You're dead without your helmet."

Without thinking, Ivan darted back out onto the street and plucked his helmet from the hot dust. The dark shadow poured like lava across the stones as a massive diabolos dropped from the sky at him, roaring so loudly it made his chest shudder. He threw himself back into the alleyway just as the thing flapped past. A near miss.

Ivan clutched his helmet with quaking, stupid fingers and clumsily pushed the piece on. Jumping into the breastplate on the ground, he yanked it up as fast as he could but found it difficult to secure the leather straps with his sweaty fingers. It didn't help that all around him the diabolon were soaring and thundering and people were screaming at the top of their lungs.

Glancing down the street, Ivan saw a line of knights trying to mount a counter-attack. "For the King," they cried. He watched the brave garrison advance on two diabolon who had made a stand in the middle of the street. He shook his head as he realized two of the knights were mere children. One was an older woman. They swung their swords wildly at the monsters, mostly tracing air.

The diabolon were not intimidated. Daggered fangs bared, the giant cat-dragons circled the knights, growling and snarling with rage, throbbing for an outlet. One beast lunged forward, teeth snapping. It locked its massive jaws over a man who was too slow of foot. Flipping the hapless warrior into the air like a chunk of meat, the thing's mouth distended unnaturally as it devoured him—armor and all—in a few greedy bites. The second monster lashed out with its formidable paws, cuffing the woman so hard that she cannoned across the street and pounded through a wooden porch. She could not have survived the blow.

The horrific sights froze Ivan's mind momentarily. Where was the King? Who would defend them against this attack? He noticed that the knights were now retreating. One was hastily limping toward his alley, dragging a badly mangled leg behind him.

"Are you all right?" Ivan asked, concerned.

"I'll live. But long live the King."

As the man spoke, Ivan winced at the sight of his blood-flecked teeth. "Does this happen often?"

"The war, you mean? Daily. It's a moment by moment crusade every true citizen of Basileia must embrace with courage. Our enemy whispers in our thoughts. He brings us sickness and tempts us to abandon the Pursuit. He attacks us with ruthless evil every day of our lives and can be lurking anywhere. For all you know, I might be one of his dark allies. The only way to survive is to fight back with everything the King provides."

"What enemy? Who are you talking about?"

"Pythus, the serpent king of Kakos. Our true enemy."

"Why doesn't the King do something about this Pythus?" Ivan asked, still terrified.

"Oh, he has. Many years ago, when the bridge between Kakos and Basileia was completed, he marched to Kakos and overcame Pythus and the diabolon all by himself. His noble victory gives us a place to stand today in battle. His victory is our victory."

Ivan looked down at the knight's leg, still bleeding critically. "It doesn't look like you're winning, or ever could for that matter. Those monsters are huge."

"A glorious day is coming when our final victory will come, but until then, we must engage the enemy and use the armor and weapons the king gives us to defeat our foes."

"I thought you said they were already defeated."

"Correct."

"But then …" Ivan had barely uttered the words when his mind registered the sound of a lion breathing to his left. A sinister diabolos was at the mouth of the alleyway, its fiery eyes narrowed with volcanic hatred.

The knight let his shield drop to his knees. "It must have sniffed out a hole in my armor." He was giving up. "They can smell weakness. I need more prayer support. Don't make my mistake."

The diabolos cackled. "We can smell much more than weakness, you paltry weed. Your carelessness ushers in your death. Your flesh will be my feast."

Astoundingly, the soldier offered no resistance to the bloodthirsty creature as it charged into the alley, thrashing him against the wall like a limp plaything. Spinning around to flee, Ivan noticed too late that he had backed himself up against the railing overlooking Level Four. As the beast charged with gaping jaws, he was plowed over the edge and plunged into space. His only thought was that if he died now, he would never see his girls again. Ivan's scream was cut short by a punishing impact a moment later.

# Chapter Six: Crash

Throbbing pain rippled through Ivan's back, neck, and hips, muted somewhat by the fierce ringing in his ears. It took a full minute to grasp what had just happened. The diabolos had flipped him off the Fifth Level and he had fallen. Fallen where? To the Fourth Level, apparently. And he wasn't dead, at least not yet. Grimacing at the pain he felt when he tried to move, he decided to stay put for the time being.

The mackerel sky hung listless above him, staring blankly at him through a hole in the thatched roof that had saved his life by breaking his fall. His armor had probably helped too, though the back of his head had a nasty bump on it. Half expecting a diabolos or even the dark lord Pythus himself to leap through the opening at any moment to finish him off, he tried to stop his heart from pounding.

The attack never came. In fact, all the sounds and screams of battle had ceased. Which meant he had been left for dead. How long had he been unconscious? Wiggling his toes, he ruled out broken legs. Next he rotated each arm, relieved that they were in working order too. His back seemed deeply bruised, but with concerted effort he managed to roll into a sitting position among the nest of straw and mortar he had dragged down with him on his way through the roof.

Next he removed his helmet, now rank from the sweat and heavy breathing of battle. This helped quell the ringing in his ears a little, but he felt a chill run through his body as the evening air spilled into his armor.

Even so, he had to get the clumsy iron off. With some effort and pain, he managed to strip the armor and stood leaning against an interior wall, breathing hard. An empty goblet lay on its side on the floor beside the table.

He had landed in the middle of his home on the Fourth Level. Was there no escape? A fresh basket of Nomothesia's apples was arranged quaintly on the kitchen table. The sight made him furious. He batted it into oblivion with the back of his hand, then stormed out of the house.

Ivan let himself rail at the King and the blank sky. "I want my life back. Following you is too much work. I can't feel you, I can't see you, and I just about got myself killed trying to follow you." Marching down the road toward the stairwell, he continued his rant. "This can't be what faith is about. If it is, I think I'll stop caring so much. Ignorance sounds like bliss. Well, maybe not bliss, but it's better than locking horns with Pythus all day. But wait, maybe this doubt is just the diabolon at work, baiting me again. Maybe I've fallen prey to their sinister devices." He laughed manically. "I'd better check my armor for holes I've overlooked. Or bellow out some more promise prayers. Or reclaim my blessings before they're gone for good." Growling to himself, he climbed the steep stairs back down to the Third Level. "No, wait. How could I be so blind? I should starve myself some more, just in case you've withdrawn from me because of some awful sin I'm not aware of. Better safe than sorry, I guess. Right?"

Ivan paused, waiting for the King to answer. "Sorry, I forgot how busy you are and how small I am in comparison. I suppose I had it coming. I haven't memorized enough of your precious book to earn another note on the table. Maybe another ten minutes a day would do the trick. Or is it twenty? I love guessing games."

Ivan began to run. "While I'm at it, maybe I should line up with Simeon at the fountain of death for my daily refill of salt water." People were staring at him, mouths agape, but he didn't care. "You should try it too. Maybe we all should. Drink up, you sorry, stupid sheep." Shouting at them didn't help, but the bitterness of his soul was bubbling to the surface and he was determined not to censor it this time. Something had snapped within him, broken deep inside. His hope had crumbled, his faith had shattered, and he wanted out. He descended the stairs to the Second Level.

"Quick, hand me another list." His voice sounded raw, like a banshee's. He didn't care. "Somebody, quick. I need more guilt. More failure. More to do, more to kill my heart. Why on earth would I want to see my wife again? Or my Sarah? No, I'd rather die here as a miserable wretch any day." He was sobbing now, and he choked on his tears.

Nomothesia stood in front of him, gripping her cart nervously. "Ivan, what's wrong?" She moved toward him, arms extended with motherly sympathy.

"What's wrong? What's not? And by the way, your mask is on crooked. I can see your sins plain as day." He shook his fist at the onlookers. "I can see all of your sins, in fact. Every single juicy one of them." He heard himself screaming, and his arms waved in threatening circles to match. Nomothesia's face went slack but he didn't care. He sprinted past her, pushing his tortured body beyond its ability to keep up. By the time he'd found the final staircase to the main level he was hyperventilating badly. Halfway down the stairs, he began to see stars.

"Old City or New City?"

The toothless lump of a guard was still there, doing his special job— handing out the Book of Despair to people who didn't know any better. He bowled the man over with special gusto, sending the brainless greeter sprawling headlong over a neat stack of his shiny new books. Ivan tried to blink away the darkness seeping into his mind, but he couldn't stop it. The blackness dripped like psychic tar into his ragged soul. Stumbling out the front gate of the accursed city, he vaguely recalled the gravelly path slipping away from his feet and the ground flying up to meet him. His face slapped the earth and everything went black.

# Chapter Seven:
## Awakening

Over the next few hours Ivan's mind registered several confusing sensations—being dragged across gravel, bouncing and jiggling, and recently the sweet aroma of freshly baked bread. It was the bread that finally coaxed him from his despondent stupor. That, and the singing. A woman was in the room with him, humming some kind of tune under her breath. He kept his eyes closed, opting to feign sleep until he had determined what was going on. The singing was his first clue. His wife? No, the voice was all wrong. Nomothesia?

Ivan instantly recalled the harsh words he had spoken to his friend and regretted even opening his mouth. Another stupid failure. Whatever mineshaft he had fallen into was his own business. She had meant nothing but good from the moment he'd met her and didn't deserve the disrespect he'd slapped her with. On the other hand, he wasn't sure he wanted to be in her company anymore. Quite simply, he'd had quite enough of the Book of Duties. The guilt it had dumped on his soul felt asphyxiating. Feeling around in his tunic, he was quite relieved to discover he had dropped the book somewhere along his manic descent. Good riddance. He just wanted to go home.

Opening his eyes just a crack, he indulged in a slow pan of the room from right to left. A quaint little cottage of some kind with a rotund woman kneading a large ball of dough several feet away. To the left—he snapped his eyes shut as they fell on a smallish figure sitting next to him. A little girl watching him like a hawk. And giggling.

"I saw you peeking. How'd you sleep?"

Ivan wouldn't have exactly called his unconscious state sleep. It had been more like a religion-induced coma. But he couldn't exactly say that, so he opened his eyes and managed a weak smile.

"Okay, I guess."

At his voice the woman turned to him, smiling warmly. "Well, hello. I see you've awakened. And my goodness. You look better already." She stood up and craned her neck out a tiny window over the sink. "Vita, our guest is awake." She saw Ivan raising an eyebrow and understood. "I'm Rosa, and Vita is my husband. He found you curled up in the fetal position outside the wall."

Ivan blushed with humiliation. "I … I just …"

"None of that." It was a gentle scolding, but then she slipped him an unpretentious smile. "That's where he found me a couple of years ago."

"Yup. It's true," the little girl said, piping in.

"Our daughter, Shelah," Rosa explained.

The front door screeched on its hinges, wobbling inward to make room for a giant man squeezing through the doorway. He had to duck a full inch just to get through. The woman motioned proudly toward him. "My Vita."

Vita's blue eyes sparkled. "And I see you've met Rosa." He strode over to Rosa, lodging an affectionate kiss on her cheek. Now it was her turn to blush.

"Are you well? Can you walk?" Vita asked Ivan.

"My back hurts. And my head, come to think of it. But sure, I guess so."

"This will help." Rosa tore off a generous chunk of the fresh bread that had wooed him from his melancholy stupor and handed it to him.

"Thank you," he said, remembering his despair. "But I have to get going."

"I found you outside of the city, friend." Vita was frowning with apparent concern. "Where have you come from? Where were you going?"

Ivan sighed for what felt like the millionth time since he had entered Basileia. "Apparently I came from Kakos, but during the past few weeks I've been giving it a go here in Basileia. I was on my way back out when you found me."

"Back to Kakos? Why?" The child's eyes looked like eggs ready to hatch.

"No, not to Kakos. Back home. But if I can't get home, then back to Kakos, onto the bridge, or maybe a one way trip to the bottom of the chasm." He let his eyes drop to the floor. "I'm done with Basileia and the Pursuit. I'm done with the King."

Glancing up at Vita, he saw that his host's eyes were brimming with tears. "You've been staying in the Old City, haven't you?"

"Most people do."

"You don't have to be defensive. What he means is that it's written all over your face," Rosa said.

"My face?"

"Your mask."

Shelah stepped closer to Ivan and took his face in her tiny hands before he could pull away. She stood there until he had worked up the courage to return her gaze. She looked and even smelled like his daughter, little Sarah. Her voice melted his bitterness a little.

"Can I take it off?"

"It must be pretty beat-up by now." Shame hung on his shoulders like a heavy yoke, but Shelah was waiting for his reply. "Go ahead."

"It doesn't even fit you anymore, silly," she said, tenderly peeling the stubborn layer off inch by inch. When she was done with it she held the skin at arm's length like it was some kind of dead animal she'd found in the yard. She quickly passed it to Vita, who flung the sticky mess into the fire. It bubbled and contracted for a minute, then his old face burst into flames.

"Good riddance," Rosa said.

"Your face still looks so sad. Don't be sad." Shelah was staring into his eyes, searching for something. And for the first time since he'd met her, her eyes looked sad too. A doleful lump began climbing his throat and he tried to chase it down again.

"I really should be going."

"No, you should stay." Rosa put her hand gently over his. "Don't write off Basileia until you have lived awhile in the New City."

"The New City?" Ivan felt his upper lip quiver. "The King mentioned the New City in some of his notes to me."

"The New City is his home," Vita said, gesturing to the world outside.

"And yours, if you'd like," Rosa added.

"Please stay with us. He can stay, right, Mama?" Shelah wiped away a tear that had slipped from his eyes. But just as suddenly as he felt himself soften, he steeled himself, hardening his heart like stone and gritting his teeth. He stood up suddenly, breaking free of the embrace. His scalp was burning with confusion again.

"No. I've tried every level this city has to offer. I've followed the rainbow you people seek all your lives, right to the very end, right into the clouds. It led me to nothing but a gaping hole in my soul. I may never see my family again."

"I don't know about your family, but you haven't tried the New City." Vita's voice was firm.

"I'm done trying," Ivan replied, his voice even firmer. "I've got to find a way to get home."

Vita sighed, gesturing toward the door. "Then we won't stop you."

"It's nothing personal. I've just had my hopes dashed too many times to count. Too often to recover from. I need to walk away. I'm done. I'll find my own way home somehow."

"I understand." Rosa was smiling through tears. The look in her eyes told Ivan she was telling the truth. Under different circumstances he would have liked to hear her story, but the awkwardness was palpable. Nodding to Vita as he stepped out of the cottage, he braced himself for a second journey out of the accursed city.

Ivan lifted his eyes to chart his path and stopped cold. His jaw dropped. His heart pounded. His skin flushed. His body trembled. A cry escaped his lips before he could even react. He stumbled back through the door. Vita, Rosa, and Shelah were standing there grinning, arms crossed, apparently waiting for him to return.

"It's ... it's ..."

"We know."

Vita extended a burly hand to Ivan. "Care to take a walk, friend?"

"Here, take some more bread." Rosa stuffed a chunk into his palm just before Vita led him out the front door into a whole new world. The King's world.

# Chapter Eight:
# The Book of Life

Ivan felt like a little child visiting a fair, the ocean, the mountains, and his grandparent's cottage—for the first time—all at the same time. He walked as if he were in a trance, trying to take in the wonders around him. He stretched out a tingling hand. The air felt alive, shimmering and twinkling as if exquisitely small golden snowflakes were suspended weightless before them. As he moved his hands, the stuff swirled like liquid, brightening momentarily wherever his hands made contact with the particles.

"What is it?"

Vita smiled warmly, also enjoying the look on Ivan's face. "It's the air of the kingdom. The glory of the King. His kingdom is a realm of light, of glory, of life."

"I can see that," Ivan replied, mesmerized at the sight. "Is it always here, or does it come and go?"

"The kingdom is a real place, Ivan. Many people forget that. A kingdom begins with a King, as you know. In the Old City, the kingdom is all about the rules and subjection. But there cannot be a kingdom without a realm. The King's realm includes the space in our hearts given over to him, but it's far more than that. The truths in the King's book are not just pretty words or novel ideas. You have entered a real kingdom, a realm of splendor and light. Bask in its glow. Breathe it in."

"I think I can handle that."

Vita laughed. "I should hope so."

"You mentioned the King's book. It seems that I threw mine away." Ivan felt a pang of regret at the thought. But it was too late now.

"Is this the one?" Vita slipped a book from behind his back. Ivan thought he recognized the worn brown cover immediately, but the title was different.

"No," he said finally.

"I found it right next to you by the Gate."

"My book was a Book of Duties."

"I supposed it was."

"This one is a Book of Life."

"At this moment, yes."

Ivan was confused. "Then it isn't mine."

"My King, help me to explain this to my friend."

"Pardon me?"

"I was talking to the King."

"Praying, you mean. Been there, done that. But not anymore."

"You haven't truly prayed until you've prayed from within the New City," Vita explained. "I also assure you that this is your book."

"No, it's got the wrong name. This one says 'The Book of Life.' Mine was a "Book of Duties."

"I know. But the book is alive, Ivan."

"Alive?"

"Yes. It contains the breath and life of the King. But all living things adapt to their surroundings, so when we touch the book our personality mingles with the message. We tend to see it as we are, not as it is. Look at the book again." He gave it to Ivan.

Ivan looked again. He cocked his head at the sight, confused. "The Book of Duties."

"Is it?"

"Sure. Look for yourself. The letters clearly say so on the cover." Ivan handed the volume back to Vita. A moment later, the big man shook his head in disagreement.

"No. It's a Book of Life. See?" Sure enough, the letters now spelled "The Book of Life," just as they had a minute earlier.

"I don't understand. Is this a trick?"

"Not a trick. A truth. For though the King's word never changes, our experience of its truths never stops changing. In a sense, the book becomes what we think it's for. Violent zealots see it as a justification for their evil, and in their hands it becomes what they see. For you, indoctrinated with the lies of the Old City, the book is a Book of Duties. But for me, filled with the life of the New City, the book is a way to enjoy the King. A Book of Life. I see it more like the King intends people to see it, so that's how I experience it."

"Well, then I want to see what you see." Ivan felt a vulnerable kind of hope flickering in his soul again. He snatched the book from Vita and stared hard at the cover. The Book of Duties. His heart sank. "I want to know the King. I want this book to be what he intended for me."

"Tell the King that."

"But he's not here."

"Just try."

Ivan sighed. "King, I want to know you, wherever you are. I want to see what Vita sees."

For a minute nothing happened. But then the cover became a thick liquid, swirling and morphing until the letters spelled *The Book of Life*. Cracking it open excitedly, he flipped through a few dozen pages, skimming the words as they flew by. The words smelled like rich food, like Rosa's fresh bread feeding his soul. The stories seemed to jump off the pages—or had he entered the book?

"Where are all the lists? Are they all gone?" His heart was racing.

"All but one." Vita pointed to the page.

Ivan read what Vita had highlighted. "Love the King and love what he loves. That's it? Just two things?"

"Actually, they're one thing. Loving the King means loving what and whom he loves. And you can spend your whole life doing that one thing. In fact, that's the point."

"I see, I see." Ivan jumped up and down, then stopped, surprised at himself. He managed a breathless nod just before an unpredictable joy split the threadbare seams of his heart, tumbling out of his mouth as childlike laughter.

"You're becoming a child again." Tears of joy welled up in Vita's blue eyes.

"What do you mean?"

"You cannot enter Basileia with a grownup heart. Nor can you experience true joy with an old heart, no matter how long you've lived here. Your joy tells me that your old heart is growing younger again. Your soul left the city without you knowing it, and now it is returning."

# Chapter Nine: Grace

Ivan awoke before the roosters and seriously considered finding one so he could scare the living feathers off it. He was tingling with excitement, ready to begin his daily readings and prayers. Time to impress the King. Unfortunately, the door screeched on its hinges as usual and he was sure he had woken the entire household, maybe even the neighbors. He sat himself down on a mat just outside the door.

"I'm here, King. I'm back. Please forgive me for my despair and all those bad things I said about you and Basileia. Help me to seek you and to find you. Oh, and to get home to Monica and Sarah. Amen."

Ivan opened his eyes and saw a tiny sparrow had landed on the mat with him. Amused, he stretched out his hand. To his surprise, the bird hopped onto his hand and stood there flitting, bobbing its head, and looking into his eyes.

Just then the door screeched again behind him. It was Shelah. The sparrow flew away, spooked by the loud noise.

"What are you doing?" Shelah looked like she was still half asleep. Her hair was plastered to her face on one side.

"I'm doing my daily readings and prayers for the King. I want to be a good citizen."

Shelah blinked slowly, apparently still trying to wake up. She yawned. "That's an Old City thing, silly."

"What do you mean?"

"Devotional correctness. That's an Old City thing. We don't do that here."

"You don't do your daily readings and prayers?" He was shocked.

"No. Why should we?"

"Because that's what the King wants. That's what we need. Every good citizen …"

"Does the Book of Life say that?"

"Sure it does!" Ivan tried to stay calm. "Lots of times. Devotional correctness is what makes you a good citizen."

"Are you sure? That sounds a lot like the Book of Duties to me."

"How can you say that? The King wrote the book for us!"

"Yup. And I love it and read it all the time. But there aren't any rules about reading it every day."

"No, it's in here. I'm positive." Ivan gave his book a firm pat.

"Well, tell me when you find it." Shelah yawned again. "King, would you please show him the truth?" She stood there looking off into space for a second. "Oh, you will? Thank you. Then I'm going back to bed."

After Shelah went back inside, Ivan's curiosity got the best of him. Scanning the book's index, he found nothing about devotional correctness or instructions for daily readings. An hour later the entire house was stirring and he still hadn't found a command or list or anything prescribing a daily devotion time like he'd practiced in the Old City. Next he searched the stories about the faith heroes and friends of the King. They were incredible warriors, lovers, poets, husbands, wives, and children—obviously favorites of the King's court—but none of them mentioned their daily devotions. They loved the King very much and talked to him often. They loved his book too. But they didn't seem to discipline themselves into a daily routine—at least not like the one he'd malpracticed in the Old City. This discovery came as a huge relief.

"Breakfast, Ivan." He didn't have to be asked twice. Whatever Rosa was cooking smelled delicious, and by this time he was ready to eat two breakfasts. After sitting down at the table he faced Shelah sheepishly. Thankfully, she waited until after breakfast to ask him about his search.

"So?" Her eyes already knew the answer.

"I couldn't find it. But it must be there."

"What must be there?" Vita asked.

"Devotional correctness, daily readings. All the routines good citizens of Basileia adopt to please the King so he can bless them."

Vita sighed. "Eat up. We've got a lot of work to do, Ivan."

Ivan inhaled breakfast and washed up. He followed his new mentor out the front door. Vita tried to lead him through the New City, but it was slow going since Ivan felt compelled to stop and take in all the beautiful sights, smells, and sounds around him. The shimmering glory of the air still astounded him. Every detail seemed to anoint him with energy and joy. Stopping to take a giant, slow breath, he cocked his head backward, lifting his hands toward the sky. "King, you've outdone yourself in the New City." Dropping his gaze, he noticed that the ground had changed under his feet since he had last looked at it. The pavement was solid and liquid at the same time, fluttering and rippling as he tested it with his feet.

"Let me guess, the ground is alive too."

Vita was already thirty paces ahead of him. The big man turned, feigning annoyance. "We really do have somewhere to go. You could work a little harder at keeping up. But in answer to your question, no, the ground is not alive."

"Then what's it made of?" Ivan squatted on his haunches to touch it with his fingers. "It looks like pavement, but it's not, is it?" The moment he made contact with the substance, shivers ran up and down his body and seemed to congregate in his heart. It was almost impossible not to smile at the sensation.

"It's pure grace, Ivan. Everywhere you go in Basileia, you're standing on the grace of the King. And you're smiling because of what grace is made of. Its essence causes joy."

"I'll say." Ivan's eyes brimmed with tears. It felt good to cry about something wonderful for a change.

"If you think that's amazing, wait until you see where we're going." Vita gently took hold of his arm and led him through the rest of the city, to its very center—a grassy hill with a lone cross on top.

"Golgotha?"

Vita didn't have to answer. In fact, he couldn't answer. This was the place where the King had given his life to pay for the sins of the citizens of Basileia and Kakos alike. It filled Ivan with dread, wonder, and thankfulness all at once.

"May we go to the top?" Ivan asked.

"May we? We must. I come back here as often as I can."

Up they went. Each step seemed holy. Every moment seemed to grow weightier and mightier than the one before it. Ivan found himself looking down at the grass, which now looked more like a stream flowing down the hill than foliage. In fact, it was a stream, a fountain covering the entire hill, glazing it in the very same grace that made up the pavement below. The stream was the grace that formed the foundation of the whole city. His eyes followed the water to its source, slowly scaling the hill until he saw the cross standing before him. He gasped in horror.

The King was on it, bleeding and dying. Turning back to face Vita with fear, he noticed that his friend's face was wet with tears. With great effort and a trembling chin, Vita spoke.

"No, the King isn't on the cross right now. But his sacrifice is eternal, which means every time we come to the cross, his blood still flows as fresh as the day it was shed. In a sense, we must all come to him and look him in the eye at this place. Until we do that, we cannot know."

"Know what?"

"You must take this journey by yourself."

Ivan found himself trembling. The King was beaten badly and blood ran freely down his ragged flesh. Cruel spikes skewered his hands and feet, pinning him to the horrific wood. He writhed in pain.

"Who did this to him?" Anger smashed through Ivan's veins.

"I did." Vita was sobbing loudly. Vita? The humble giant? But then another voice sounded, a voice so gentle it was powerful beyond words.

"You did too, Ivan." The voice of the King. And there was no arguing with the King.

"I did," he said, hating himself.

"Look at me." The King was speaking to him. The King he had been searching for. The King he had rejected in the Old City. Trembling violently now, his eyes and nose flowing like the hill, shame and guilt wracked his body with physical pain. Ivan looked up. He met the King's gaze. Looked right into his eternal eyes.

They were Genesis, and they were Revelation. The sea and the stars. Sunrise and sunset, beginning and end. They were soaring joy and crushing sadness. Roaring thunder and gentle breeze. Fire and snow. And they were love. Pure, raging, unmaking, resurrecting, searing, scarring, dancing love—for him. Ivan felt like he was being drawn into the King's very soul. His eyes spun out a magnificent whirlpool of spirit and life.

"Give me your list." The King spoke again but no longer from the cross. He now stood next to Ivan, hand outstretched. The cross stood bare before them—cold, rough, and crude.

Ivan didn't understand. "What list, my King?"

"The one in your hand."

The one in his hand. How could he have missed it earlier? The damning, endless list of do's and don'ts, the thickening list of his endless failures, the list of duties and laws and rules he could never keep. The death of his passion. That list.

"Give it to me, Son."

Ivan gave the King the thick stack of paper in slow motion, as if in a trance. An infernal weight lifted from his soul a moment later and he wondered whether he weighed anything at all. But the trance was broken with a "Bang!" so loud that it rang in his ears. He nearly jumped out of his skin when he saw what the King was doing. Bang! He was nailing the accursed list to the cross. Bang! Pounding it with all his might, grunting with a fierce anger that nearly seemed unbecoming of the King. Bang! Almost. The list shriveled right there on the cruel wood, flaking and rotting and flaming and shrinking—and then the crossbeam itself seemed to eat both the nail and then the list, sucking it right into the core.

It was gone. The ghastly list was gone.

Now what?

Ivan slept soundly that night, better than he had in weeks. He woke to find Shelah standing on her tiptoes next to his mattress, her angelic face hovering just six inches from his own. She was up to something. "Good morning, sleepyhead."

Ivan groaned. "You got to sleep in yesterday. Go away."

"And you slept in today."

Ivan stretched his arms above his head. "What time is it?"

"Time for lunch."

"Lunch?" He sat up with a start. "Did I sleep that long?"

"Just kidding." Shelah poked him in the ribs, bounding back from the bed like a playful rabbit. If she wanted a game, a game she would get. Ivan erupted from the mattress, hands poised like claws with fingers wiggling.

"Are you ticklish?"

She screamed in delight, scampering through the house with Ivan close on her heels.

"Children, time to clean up for breakfast," Rosa called out sternly. She reached out to snag Ivan's collar as he ran by. "That includes adults who haven't grown up," she scolded, one eyebrow raised in feigned disapproval.

"Hey, Vita said I had to become like a little child again."

"Childlike and childish are not the same thing. Now wash up."

"Yes, Mother." Ivan grinned at her and she returned the smile.

After washing up together in the metal basin and getting each other thoroughly wet, Ivan and Shelah sat down together at the breakfast table, trying not to laugh. Breakfast was delicious, but with Vita around he didn't have much time to relish the moment.

"Let me guess, it's time for a walk."

Ivan was getting used to the walks. And depending on them, actually. After Vita had kissed Rosa, and Ivan had chased down Shelah to plant a peck on her cheek, the two men pushed through the screeching door and walked outside. Playing with Shelah made his heart throb with longing for his little Sarah.

"When can I meet the King, Vita?"

Vita's eyes sparkled again. "Today, Ivan. Today."

They were just twenty paces from the house when Ivan stopped in his tracks.

"Again?" Vita teased, pretending to be disgusted.

But Ivan didn't dignify the jab. Something had been nagging at him through his dreams during the night. Vita had led him to Golgotha the previous afternoon. Right in the middle of the city. Which made no sense—Basileia was built onto a mountain.

"Where is it? Where is the mountain? And the Old City? And all the levels?"

"There are no levels in Basileia."

"Very funny. I climbed them. I lived on them. I even fell from one."

"An Old City illusion devised to make the privileged few feel self-righteous. The ground is level in the New City. There is no climb, no ascending to the King. He lives among us. And when you come to fully live here, the Old City loses its appeal. Soon after that, it vanishes entirely."

"Yeah, it's pretty great. But I have to say, I sure miss the apples."

Vita scrunched up his face. "Pardon me?"

"The apples. I pretty much lived on them in the Old City."

"Ah, Nomothesia." Vita shook his head.

"You know her?"

"Sure I know her."

"Her apples are delicious, aren't they? And they made me hungry for the book."

"Did she ever tell you where she got them?"

"I never thought to ask."

"Every morning she leaves Basileia to collect them outside the gates."

"Outside?"

"Come, I'll show you." He started walking again, and as usual, Ivan was taking his time. "Today, Ivan." He waved his companion forward. Ivan followed, still gawking at the shimmering world around him, chuckling at the grace lining the streets. Fifteen minutes later they were approaching the city gate.

"I don't want to leave," he said. "I mean, I want to go home, to see my family."

"I know. We aren't leaving. Trust me."

Toothless Joe cowered behind the cart as they approached, but Ivan extended his hand. "Sorry about the other day."

Looking first to Vita for reassurance, he took Ivan's hand and shook it. "That's okay. Old City or New City?"

Ivan laughed. "New City, definitely." The man held out a book. A Book of Life. "No, I'm good, thanks."

Pulling Ivan by the arm, Vita stepped through the gate. He pointed to a rough spot on the gravel just outside. "That's where I found you the other day."

Ivan smiled. He had come a long way, hadn't he?

"Here we are."

"At the bridge?"

"At the bridge."

Ivan stood looking out over the chasm. "What am I supposed to be looking at, exactly?"

"First of all, that big tree over there. That's where your friend gets her apples." A tree with a trunk thicker than a barrel and a crown wider than a house stood to the left of the gate. Sure enough, it was laden with the apples he'd lived on the past few weeks. Some of the branches were so full of fruit that they had bent over until they were resting on the ground.

"Oh, man. Can I pick some? I've got a craving."

"If you'd like."

Ivan walked up to the tree and paused there, standing in its shadow. He was about to pluck a big apple when he was startled by a rustling sound above him. Before he could react, a slender snake with cruel fangs dropped its head from the foliage. The reptile was bright green, the same shade as the apples. Ivan cried out, then jumped back.

"What on earth?!"

"It's the Tree of Knowledge."

"Are you serious? Didn't God remove it from the Garden of Eden when Adam and Eve were banished?" He was now standing next to Vita several paces back from the Tree.

"No, Ivan. He transplanted the Tree of Life in Basileia, but the Tree of Knowledge just adapted, splitting off into a thousand different forms and sending its greedy roots into every corner of society. True knowledge is not just for the mind, but the heart. It comes from friendship with the King. Even the Book of Life isn't an end in itself. It is designed to lead us past itself to him."

"Isn't Nomothesia worried about the snake? What if it bites her?"

"She's already been bitten, Ivan. But enough of that. Take a look at the bridge." Ivan looked.

"I am. It's impressive."

"Keep looking. Does it look familiar to you?"

"Well, not …" Ivan began, then stopped. He looked at the bridge again. The span, the spire, the supporting pillar just beneath it. Then it struck him. He gasped. "It's a giant cross!"

"Not a cross. The cross. And what's it doing?"

"Bridging?"

"Yes. Between Kakos and Basileia. Between the old life and the King."

"Which is how I got here. I get that."

"But where is here?" Vita's eyes flashed with passion. Ivan didn't grasp his line of thought, and Vita saw it. "In the Old City you spent every waking hour engaged in the Pursuit. Why?"

"Because the King wants us to seek him. Because I wanted to get closer to him. To find him. So I could get back home."

"And?"

Ivan felt his eyes mist over, then fill with tears. "I got a few notes and found a footprint here and there. But that was all. It was so frustrating."

"It nearly killed Rosa too. I found her collapsed outside the gate years ago, very close to the spot where I found you. That was ten years ago, before we married."

"She's a beautiful woman, Vita. You're a lucky man."

"Do you know why she's so beautiful?"

Ivan shook his head.

"Because she's living in the secret I'm about to show you." Ivan desperately wanted what Rosa had. She reminded him of his Monica.

Vita turned to stand face to face with him and gripped his tightly. "You must listen very closely. You cannot ever get closer to King."

Ivan's heart sank. But it was true. "I … I know." His lip quivered with emotion. He would never get back home, would he? His hope was all but gone.

"No. Ivan, you cannot ever get closer to the King. All the hide and seek of the Old City is futile. There is nothing a mortal can ever do to ascend into his presence. There is nothing any of us can do to bridge this chasm." The telltale twinkle flashed in the man's eye again. Ivan just stood there, numb. His brain wasn't following yet. "Ivan, there is nothing any mortal can do. But the King can draw near to us. The King can bridge the chasm. And as you can see, he's already done it."

Ivan furrowed his brow. "That's it? That's your secret? I know that already. That's how I was delivered from Kakos. But once we're here in the city, it's different. All good citizens must engage in the Pursuit."

"The Pursuit is real, but you have it backwards."

"Backwards?"

"The King is pursuing us. He bridged the chasm to bring us near. To bring himself near. So we never have to seek him again."

Never seek the King? Ivan felt something in his heart shift. A kernel of faith sprang into existence as they stepped out onto the bridge.

"He's given himself to us, Ivan. Fully and forever."

Another kernel of faith popped. His vision began to swirl.

"He's right there above you. Look."

Ivan nearly choked on his surprise. The King was hovering there above him, filling the sky with his splendor.

"He's in front of you, Ivan."

And there he was, majestic and smiling broadly. Right in front of him.

"And all around you."

He truly was. Everywhere, all around him.

"And behind you."

Ivan was about to spin around to look when he felt a strong hand rest on his shoulder from behind. A hand graced with a royal ring. A hand scarred deeply through the palm. Ivan bit his lip as giant tears spilled down his cheeks. Vita stepped back, nodded reverently at the King, and walked cheerfully toward home.

"Vita is a true brother," the King said. "But now I am with you."

.d he crumpled into a spasmodic joy. The glory
. him. The grace on the bridge rippled as he fell.
.th you." Those last words rumbled like thunder,
core. He looked down and saw the King there too,
,m within the bridge, filling it, holding him up. In fact,
.e bridge.

.n he thought he might explode with wonder, the King
abo. , around him, in front of him, behind him, and beneath him
multipn.d somehow, the originals remaining exactly as they were but part
of them moving toward him like resplendent currents of vitality. And then
they charged inside his body, melting into his frame, becoming one with
his spirit. His body snapped rigid, full of power and glory. Ivan was sure
his eyes were on fire, though he felt no pain.

"Ivan, my son, my child, I am in you, and you are in me, and I am
in my Father." The words came from the King's heart, and they felt like
a thunderclap. The sound pushed deep cracks through many of the Old
City lies within him. He could sense them buckling under the explosive
strain of the King's presence. Then they shattered into a million pieces
and evaporated.

"Do not seek me, Ivan," the King said, whispering now. "Never again.
You already have me. Do not pursue me; enjoy me. Do not chase after me;
let me catch you. From this moment forward, let my presence transcend
both faith and feelings. Let this truth become a deep knowing that never
wavers no matter what happens around you."

"Yes, my King."

Ivan slipped into a prostrate position there on the bridge, lying flat on
his face for a very long time. The sensation of the King's indwelling was so
sublime and intense that he could hardly stand it.

"I will never seek you again," he said, weeping. "Never. Thank you,
thank you, thank you."

The King's own heartbeat was throbbing in Ivan's chest, pounding
with joy. Incredibly, he sensed that the King was as happy as he was.
Maybe more. He lay there all day watching the sun complete its course
across the sky.

# Chapter Ten: Quenched

Vita let Ivan catch up with his soul the next morning. "There's only so much transformation a person can take," he explained. Even so, Ivan was itching to explore the New City. Later in the morning he decided to take a walk on his own.

The King thought it was a fantastic idea. "May I come along?"

Ivan chuckled. "You're everywhere. I can't go anywhere without you."

"Ah, you're catching on. But you can go anywhere you wish without noticing me."

"And I used to be very good at that. But not anymore. I love this new way, where I can talk to you any time I want."

"And where I can talk to you any time I want. I dwell in every soul that makes me King, but most people don't realize it and go their whole lives without acknowledging my presence within them."

"They waste their time on the Pursuit."

"Truly. Why spend your time seeking something you already have?"

Ivan felt a pang of loneliness. The King read his expression.

"You miss your family."

Tears welled up in his eyes. "I've been trying to find a way back home for weeks now. I got so excited about your presence on the bridge yesterday that I forgot to ask you about that."

"That was why you sought me so fervently. Why you memorized scripture. Why you drank so much water from the spring."

Ivan nodded, ashamed. The King knew everything. "I'm so sorry. I just wanted to go home."

The King strode up to him and clasped his shoulders with his regal hands. "I will not allow myself to be used, Ivan."

At those words the tears spilled from Ivan's eyes onto his cheeks, running down until they collected on the tip of his chin. The King gently reached out and wiped them away.

"Do you still want to go home?"

Ivan nodded. "More than anything."

"I can send you back right now if you'd like. But I must tell you, it would sadden me very much. I'm not finished with you here yet, Ivan. But the choice is yours. It's always yours."

Ivan felt ill. He had just been given the freedom to choose his family on one hand and the King on the other. Standing there in front of him, knees knocking together and blood draining from his face, he suddenly felt nauseous. He collapsed at the King's feet, clutching the golden sandals with desperate hands.

"King, please. Don't do this to me. It's not fair." His tears were soaking the King's feet. Glancing up at the King's face, he saw the unyielding truth. He wanted to be chosen above everyone and everything, even above his girls. There was no way around it. The King would honor Ivan's choice, but he would not back down from the invitation.

"Then … I'm going to need to think about it."

"I will come by first thing tomorrow to hear your decision."

Ivan tossed and turned in his bed that night, dizzied by the tension he felt in his soul. All that night his thoughts spun in vicious circles. The decision was too difficult. How could he live without Monica and Sarah? He couldn't bear to think of losing them. How could the King be so cruel? It felt like choosing between life and death, but in this case both paths meant the death of something painfully precious.

After hours of agonizing, one simple thought seemed to settle amidst the maelstrom of confusion: Monica would never want him to choose her over the King. Never. Ivan groaned in agony with that realization. He pounded the grace lining the wall next to his cot. There was only one right thing to do, and he hated it with every fiber in his being. Worse, he hated himself for hating it. Trembling with fear, he heard himself speak the awful words.

"I … suppose I'll stay."

"I did not ask what you suppose." The King's voice was tender but firm.

A moment later Ivan found himself lying flat on his stomach on the brink of the chasm between Kakos and Basileia. Both of his arms were pulled taut over the edge, straining to hold onto something. He was horrified to realize that in one hand he gripped Monica, and in the other, his little Sarah. Both of his girls dangled over the dark abyss, held fast only by his stubborn will.

He was shocked to find that their eyes were not brimming with fear, but with tranquil love.

"Let us go, sweetheart."

Ivan's heartbeat nearly cracked his own ribs at the thought. "No, Monica. Never." Ivan gritted his teeth as his rigid body slipped an inch forward toward the chasm. His arms burned with the strain.

"Trust me, Ivan." The King was with him, hand on his shoulder.

"I can't let them go. I can't." He had to save them, not let them go. Pulling with all his might, screaming with frustration, he found he couldn't move them an inch, never mind back up over the edge. His panic became a boiling rage. He slipped another few inches forward. "I'll never let go, girls. Never." He tried to dig his feet into the grass, but couldn't find anything to stop his sliding.

"Daddy, it's okay." Her eyes shone with faith.

"No, Sarah."

"Trust me, Ivan."

Oh, he wanted to. He wanted to trust the King more than anything. He turned to look into the King's face, now wet with tears like his. "King, please help me. I can't pull them up, but I can't let them go."

"I am helping you. Trust me."

His eyes locked with the King's again, and something wondrous and terrifying passed between them. In a moment too awful to describe, the King's words suddenly jumped to life within him. They just clicked. And with the faith came peace. He turned to face the girls. Their eyes were still clear, full of the same stillness he now felt. Everything seemed to slow down—his heartbeat, his breathing, his mind.

"Honey, I have to let you go."

Monica smiled. "I know."

He let go.

Ivan awoke from the dream drenched with sweat and with the King standing at his bedside. Not just the King, but in a deeper way than ever before, *his* King. The giant monarch said nothing at first, but offered Ivan his hand and lifted him to his feet. As soon as they were standing together, he embraced Ivan heartily, nearly crushing him with his kingly strength. Ivan closed his eyes again, drinking in the deep affection. He felt the King kiss his forehead. He smelled the King's sweet breath.

"Thank you, Ivan. He who loses his life will find it."

A minute later he felt the King relax his grip and let go of the hug. When Ivan opened his eyes he saw him standing back, rubbing his hands together with great relish. "Now, my son, why go hungry and thirsty when you can be satisfied?" Ivan shook his head, trying to switch gears after what had just happened. Truth be told, he felt like he'd just been hit by a bus.

Rosa stepped into the conversation. "I beg your pardon, but I see where this is going. Could you please take this outside?"

"No, no, do it inside." Shelah stood nearby as well. She clapped her hands with glee. Rosa shot her a look.

"Do what?" Ivan looked to his friends to clarify, but they ignored him.

"He's the King, Rosa. If he wants to do it inside, let him do it." Vita smiled broadly.

"Of course I'll let him do it, Vita. I'm just asking. There's no harm in asking, is there? Why make a mess if we can do it outside?"

The King strode over to Rosa, robes flowing regally behind him. He took her face in his hands and then bent over to kiss her on the cheek. "If you would prefer we take it outside, we'll take it outside. This time, at least."

"What? What are you talking about?" Ivan realized he was shouting because everyone turned to look at him. He was embarrassed but held their gaze. "What?"

"Take it outside," they said, bursting into raucous laughter. The King took Shelah by the hand. "Would you like to help me, my love?"

"Help you? Oh, yes!" She jumped up and down like a pogo stick. "I'll help. I'll help."

The moment the King let her go she bolted across the room and clamped onto Ivan. "Come with me," she said, giggling again. Ivan was still bewildered, but let her yank him out the screeching door before he could protest. The King followed her until she had led them about twenty feet away from the house.

"Here. Yup. We'll do it right here."

The King smiled broadly. "Well done, Shelah. Now Ivan, I have something to give you. Or rather, I've already given it to you, but you don't realize it yet. And as you've already seen, most of my gifts don't become real to you until you realize they are."

Ivan nodded. He couldn't imagine what the King might still have in store. He just stood there, stately and silent, for a full minute. Incredibly, so did Shelah.

"Do you thirst for me, Ivan?"

"Yes, King." A lump rose in his throat. "I thirst for you more than anything in the universe."

"Would you like me to give you a drink?"

"A real drink, not like the fountain of death in the Old City? A drink like the ones you left for me on the table in my old house?"

"Better," the King answered. "The best drink I could give you there was like desert sand compared to what I can give you here."

"I want it." Ivan clenched his fists. "More than anything."

"Then Shelah must show you the fountain. A fountain that never stops flowing. A fountain that you can come to any time you want. A fountain of life, the water of my Spirit. Would you like to drink in my Spirit, Ivan?"

"Trust me. You do." Shelah's eyes shone brightly.

Ivan nodded, then began to tremble, as though the deepest parts of him were coming undone. His teeth started chattering. His knees knocked together. "You would share that fountain with me?"

"I hold nothing back." The King winked at Shelah.

"Now?" she asked.

"Yes, princess. Now. Show him the spring."

Biting her lip, Shelah tried to keep a straight face. She turned and walked right up to Ivan. She inched closer until she was standing six inches from him, her little heart beating like a drum. He could hear her excited breathing.

"The spring. The spring."

"Yes?"

"The spring is … right … here." And with that, she reached up, standing on her tippy-toes, and planted her little palm in the middle of his chest.

Ivan stumbled back. Something rumbled within him. Shelah was laughing again, spinning and jumping in circles. "The spring, the spring, it makes me sing," she shouted. The King began to dance with her, but the next moment everything became a blur.

A floodgate had opened inside him. From the very pit of his emptiness, from the hollow of hollows within him, sprang a torrent of fresh, cool water.

"What …" His question was cut short as the water explurted like a geyser from his mouth, from his fingertips, out of his toes, chest, and even from the top of his head.

"Hallelujah!" He screamed it again. "Hallelujah!" Then he danced madly in circles as the water sloshed everywhere, soaking the King, dousing Shelah, and even spraying through the window to spatter Rosa. A special touch from the King.

"Keep it outside." Rosa laughed heartily and a moment later she and Vita had joined the water party. Water was flowing out of all of them, forming a bubbling pool of delicious refreshment on the stones around the dwelling. Ivan saw that the King was a virtuoso of Spirit and Life.

"I love it." Ivan jumped up and down with Shelah. "I love you, King." A few moments later the flow decreased some, enough for him to be able to talk properly again.

The King's eyes were brimming with childlike wonder and love. "Now, then, are you thirsty for me, Ivan?"

Ivan stopped short, soaking wet and speechless. The whole family paused in silence, marking the moment with a holy reverence.

"Thirsty? I … well … no. Not at all. Nor can I imagine ever being thirsty again. How could I be, if the spring of your Spirit is flowing from within me?"

"How can you indeed," the King replied, laughing. "You have spent much of your life trying to fill the void in your soul."

"And now you've filled it for me."

"Actually, I filled it the moment you stepped across the bridge into Basileia. But the Old City kept that blessing hidden from you. With the spring of living water within you, you will not have to fill yourself up with anything. Not even me. Just accept this as your new reality."

"Will it always flow like this? This powerful, this satisfying?"

"Always," Vita said, putting his arm around him.

"But it won't always be so visible or emotional," the King said. "And there will be special times when I pour out even more of my Spirit on you. Or rather, you will experience more."

"Thank goodness it's not always this messy." Rosa was already sweeping the wet stones, pushing the water down a drain.

"What's wrong with messy? Some of my best work is messy," the King said.

"I'll say." Ivan sighed. And for the first time since crossing the bridge, he felt complete.

# Chapter Eleven: Rhythm

Over the next few weeks Ivan spent nearly all day, every day with the King, asking him questions, thanking him for the new life and the New City, pouring out his heart in worship and thanksgiving. In turn, the King answered many questions about the new life and the New City. Vita and Rosa often joined them, along with many friends and neighbors. Ivan loved the deep sense of community that emerged so naturally from their common bond with the King. Today, however, he and the King were alone—which was good, because Ivan had another question for him.

"Now that you crucified the list and ended the Pursuit and quenched my thirst, I'm not sure how to follow you. Or even what to do with myself. In the Old City it seemed so clear."

"And dead."

"Yes, and dead. But what now? Those routines are all I know."

"Routines are the Old City counterfeit for healthy rhythm."

"Meaning?"

"Well, every day with me will be different, and should be. We have a relationship now, a friendship, do we not?"

"Yes. And I love it."

"And what would happen to our friendship if we did the same things in the same order at the same time in the same place every single day? What if we made it a routine? A discipline? An expectation? What if we spent each day trying to recapture what we did the day before?"

about that. "I suppose it would get stale after a while."

Taking Ivan's hand, the King led him to a curious all to their left. "Look here." His eyes were twinkling the other way around? Either way, Ivan obeyed. He to the window and peered inside. Before him lay a broad garden. The flowers and foliage were bursting with life. It was magnificent.

"Hey, I've never seen this garden here before. Or the window, for that matter. Were they here before?"

The King gave his shoulder a gentle squeeze. "No, they weren't. And both will be gone tomorrow, like many of the moments I give you."

"But this is great. I want to come back here."

"I know you do. So many people stumble onto a precious moment with me and try to reproduce it by doing the same things over and over again. To be honest, they aren't the only ones that get tired of those games. I'm much more original than that, and you must let me be original with you. Windows open and close. Each of my sunsets is unique. No moment is ever repeated. Every blade of grass, every snowflake, every sunrise, every storm, everything I create is given a magic all its own."

"What does that mean for me?"

"If you let me guide you, I will lead you through a lifetime of special moments. They will seem mostly random to you, but they're anything but. Every one of them is part of my strategic plan. Sometimes I will lie you down in green pastures. Sometimes our path will meander next to still waters. Every day's journey opens up a different section of trail with unique challenges and blessings, for my sake as much as yours. Some days are dark, and will move us through pain and even death. But we'll always be together. I'll be continuously blessing you, making your spring overflow. Wherever you are, you'll be leaving a glistening trail of goodness and love behind you like a path of clues for others to find so they can enter my life too. And through it all, you'll be alive in my presence and I in yours."

Ivan shook his head. "Wow. That's so different from what I'm used to. I was taught that repetition grew godliness, that practice made perfect. But that was our idea more than yours, wasn't it?"

"Yes. But every encounter I initiate is a divine encounter. Has one day been alike since you came to the New City?"

Ivan laughed. "Not even close."

"Well, that will continue if you walk with me. Quite often I'll open the Book of Life and read to you and it will literally jump to life in your hands. Other times we'll just talk as we are now. Sometimes we'll walk, sometimes we'll share a meal, or watch my creatures at play. Other days we'll venture into Kakos to show people the way of life or spend the day helping others."

"But don't I need my routines to stay on track?"

"On track with what? Your sense of accomplishment? The list I crucified? What are you measuring? How much time you spend studying my word each day? How many verses you memorize? What people think of you? Drop the priginometry, the empty math of pride. Just walk with me. I will guide you through special seasons of focus designed to grow your faith as I see fit."

"So there will still be a structure of sorts?"

"Of course, but it will be my structure. The most important rhythms are mine to command, not yours. Night and day, the seasons, your heartbeat, your breathing, and the growth of your soul. Your spiritual development isn't up to you. Self-discipline does not produce passion; passion produces self-discipline." He put his hands on Ivan's shoulders and looked at him longingly. His kingly gaze held an earnest sadness that broke Ivan's heart.

"What's wrong? Have I hurt you somehow?"

"I'm real, Ivan."

"I know that."

"Then treat me that way. Let me grow you. I will always give you what you need when you need it. Don't live as if I don't exist or cannot guide you. Walk with me every day. Be completely open to what I want in every moment."

"I can do that," Ivan said, nodding.

"No, you can't. But that's all right. I don't need perfection from you. And you'll improve over time."

"I'll do my best, then."

"No you won't, not always. But I'll work with what you give me. By the way, did you enjoy the sparrow?"

Ivan smiled. "The one that landed on my knee?"

"I told him to find you. To share my smile with you. Think of him as a love note from my heart to yours."

"I felt it. Thank you." Ivan paused, trying to find words for his next question. "Why do people live in the Old City at all? Why the Book of Duties, why the list, why the guilt, the Pursuit, the hungering, thirsting, pining, and fighting? I don't get it."

For the first time since he had met the King, Ivan noticed a sad, salty tear well up in his eyes and trickle down his great cheek. "There are many reasons, and all of them break my heart. People don't want to give me control. They try to use me, as you did. They want power for themselves. It makes them feel righteous and significant to check things off a list, even if it's the wrong one. That way they can measure their growth against what other people are doing. They focus on what makes them feel good about themselves. What makes them look more spiritual."

"Instead of what makes you happy."

"Exactly. Structure seems safer, more predictable, more controllable. When it comes to faith, most Basileians choose dutiful routine over passionate relationship. But as you can see now, the power in our relationship lies in its flux, not in its structure. Structure kills the power of surprise, which is one of my favorite tools."

The King suddenly stopped, and took Ivan's elbow in his hands. "Look." Ivan looked. A young boy was tottering along a high fence, balancing as best he could. But not well enough.

"Boys will be boys."

Without warning, the boy lost his footing and fell headlong from the fence, smacking the back of his skull on the cobblestone street. Ivan gasped.

"King! That boy!"

The King was already beside the young lad. "Come here, Ivan."

Ivan obeyed. "Is he breathing? I can't see him breathing." Ivan was frantic. "We have to help him."

"I am helping him. Come closer."

Ivan obeyed again.

"Put your hand on the back of his head." Again Ivan obeyed, and nearly recoiled in shock at the swelling mass he felt growing there.

"Tell him to wake up."

Ivan did as he was told. "Wake up." Ivan could hardly think, and fearful tears rimmed his eyes. He glanced up at the King, who didn't look worried at all. A moment later Ivan's heart fluttered as the awful swelling melted away like butter on a skillet. And then the little boy woke up, flailing and gasping for air. Ivan stepped back, shocked beyond words.

The boy jumped to his feet and skittered down the street, apparently none the worse for wear.

"How ... how did I?"

"You didn't. I did it through you."

"But …"

The King laughed. "But what?"

"I didn't pray."

"No, you didn't."

"But don't I have to pray and fast for things like that to happen? In the Old City …"

The King smiled. "Ivan, miracles don't come from prayer. They come from cooperating with my Spirit in the world. Faith is a dialogue of obedience that takes many forms. Sometimes it becomes a prayer. Sometimes it becomes a hug, a meal, a shoulder to cry on, a healing moment, or even a courageous stand for justice. If you pray when I want you to act, that prayer is useless. If you act when I want you to pray, you are acting in your own strength."

"But …"

"No buts. You can do anything if you listen to my voice and do what I tell you. That, Ivan, is one of the most important lessons of the kingdom. And it's also why no two days with me are alike. My Spirit is like wind, blowing freely. If you listen to me, you will be like the wind, too."

"But if every day is different, how do I make sure I balance all the things I'm supposed to be doing?"

"You don't." That stopped Ivan in his tracks.

"I don't?"

"No. For two reasons. First of all, balancing all those things is my job. Trust me. If you walk with me, you'll never lack anything. Ever. But the second reason is that I've never asked you to be balanced. At least, not when it comes to our relationship."

"You didn't?"

"No. I asked you to be passionate. To be wholly mine, to love me. And passion is one of the most unbalanced forces in the universe. That's why I love it. Many things just can't get done within the prison of balance. And as for your devotional times, you don't need a balanced spiritual meal from me every day. That's not how I have ordered things. Consider the rhythm of nature. Seasons come and go. Fruits and vegetables all have their seasons. The rhythms of the earth provide a balanced diet over time, not a balanced meal every day. When balance and routine become too important, you begin to serve them instead of me. Without being rescued by passion, your love will eventually wither under the embalming staleness of duty. Which is why you nearly died there in the Old City.

You ensconced yourself within an empty way of life I never asked you to embrace."

"I sure did," Ivan reflected on his failures. "I guess I didn't know any better."

"Well, you do now."

Ivan nodded. He sure did. But out of nowhere, he was struck by a homesick pang that sat in his stomach like a lead ball.

"King, please don't be insulted by my asking, but am I ever going to get back home?"

"You're already home."

"No, I mean my real home."

The King smiled, raising an eyebrow. He was about to say something, but stopped himself. Ivan dropped the question for the time being. What a day.

# Chapter Twelve: Victory

Several weeks into his life in the New City, Ivan was already learning the new rhythms of passion. He learned to drink in the glory of the kingdom. He learned how to find his footing on grace, walk with the King, talk with the King, and listen to the King—though their intimacy felt like the most natural thing in the world. He never thirsted for the King again. How could he, with the spring of life within him?

Once a week he joined the throng of other Basileians who gathered at the temple, but it was nothing like the tepid cloisterings of the Old City dwellers. This was a fellowship of satisfied souls enjoying encouragement and camaraderie, a celebration of grace and the presence of the King among them. It felt wonderful to worship when the King was sitting right there among them. Ivan's love for him grew deeper with every passing day. He missed his family, but he had made his choice. He would follow the King wherever he led him.

One day the King found Ivan reclining with Vita and his friends as they studied the Book of Life together in the park.

"Hello. I'm here for Ivan."

Ivan looked at Vita.

"Go, my friend. When the King comes for you, you don't hesitate."

Ivan got up and followed the King. It struck him that he rarely knew where he was going anymore. But it didn't matter, because he knew who he was following.

"I have a very special place to show you today, Ivan," The King's face was full of regal pride again. Whenever the King had that look, something amazing was about to happen.

"Where is it?" Ivan laughed. "Let me guess. It's within me."

The King laughed with him. "No, not within you. But always with you. Turn around."

Ivan turned. Standing tall before him was a magnificent building with grand archways. Its most curious feature was the absence of doors of any kind. The whole structure was open from every side and had seemingly appeared out of thin air.

"What is it?"

"My royal treasury."

Ivan was speechless. Inside the building were countless piles of shimmering treasures, a buffet of wealth and wonder beyond Ivan's wildest imaginings. A dozen trees laden with astounding fruit ringed the outer fringes of the room. He had never seen such riches. Basileians were coming and going through the gates in a constant stream. Those who were leaving were carrying out fruit and treasures by the sackful.

"What are they carrying?" Ivan asked.

"Blessings. The riches in glory I share with you without cost. Everything you see here is yours to enjoy. Every need you have in life has a blessing to match it in my treasury, and it is my joy to give you every one of them."

"Don't people abuse that? I mean, don't they take more than they need or steal other people's blessings?"

"If you delight in me, I will shape your desires, Ivan. And besides, none of the blessings you see there belong to others."

Ivan's eyes widened. "All that is mine?"

"All of it. But not all at once. Leave the timing to me."

"And all I have to do is ask?"

"Sometimes you have to ask. But not always. Mostly you just have to trust me."

"What do you mean?"

"What kind of King and Father would I be if I only gave you what you needed when you asked for it? I don't share my treasures with you because you ask. I share them because I love you."

"In the Old City they told me to claim things. To remind you about what you promised and insist on it until I got what I asked for."

The King sighed. "Ivan, in the Old City, they don't really pray, they prayer-monger. It hurts me more than you know. Trust my heart, Ivan. My treasury is always only full of blessings fit for the child who needs them."

Ivan had to ponder that. "So when any of us come, it only holds our own blessings?"

"Yes. Unless of course you come to get something to share."

"And it's always there for all of us, individually, all at the same time?" Ivan's head was spinning.

"I have blessed you with every spiritual blessing here in the heavenly realm, Ivan."

Ivan sat down, totally overwhelmed. "Is that where I am? In the heavenly realm?"

"You are in two places at one time. I have made you a spiritual being with a physical body. Your body walks the earth while your spirit traverses Basileia. All my blessings are here, waiting for you to find them and use them in the physical realm. I've given you faith as the river through which the riches of this realm can flow into the other."

Ivan's pulse was racing. "I'm in two places at once?"

The King nodded and put his hand on Ivan's shoulder. "And today, we will visit Kakos."

"Can Vita come?"

"He's already there."

Ivan felt his pulse quicken. "Then we have to go and help him. The diabolon will eat him alive."

"We are there now too, Ivan."

He looked around, his eyes darting down at the ground, at the swirling gold-dusted air, then back at the King. "I don't understand."

"And therefore, you do not see."

"Then help me see, my King."

"Very well." The King reached out and touched Ivan's eyes. "Look up." Ivan looked up. He gasped at the sight. All around him the New City still stood, shining and majestic—but the space was shared by dark buildings, pillars of rank smoke, and soaring diabolon.

"An invasion. We must fight. We must push them back." Turning to the King, he tugged at his shoulder. "I need my armor."

"Ivan, I am your armor. I am the salvation that guards your mind. I am the righteousness that protects your heart. I am the truth that girds your loins and keeps your spiritual balance. I am the readiness that prepares you for anything Kakos can throw at you. I give you the words that can cut the enemy to pieces. Believing these things will become your shield against whatever the enemy tries to do to you. Do you believe this?"

The fire in the King's eyes was enough for Ivan. "Totally. I believe it with all my heart."

"Then you are already dressed in armor fit for a King." And it was so. Ivan was suddenly outfitted with armor so marvelous that he felt sheepish even wearing it. "Another wonderful gift." He bowed to the King.

"And as for the diabolon, they are not invading anything. This is their home, for now at least."

"No, that can't be. This is Basileia." Ivan's tension was rising because of the circling monsters, now roaring loudly as they flapped their reptilian wings through the streets of the city.

"Yes, it is Basileia. But my city, even my New City, is established right in the midst of Kakos."

"But the bridge? The cross?"

"They are real, Ivan. My sacrifice is the bridge a person must cross between cities. But Kakos and Basileia are also spiritual cities overlaying both each other and the physical world. I will show you more of this later. For now, I will show you how to deal with these enemies."

"I'll fight them if you want me to," Ivan said, trembling with fear but enflamed with loyalty for the King. But the King had vanished. He was nowhere to be seen. And just as suddenly, one of the circling diabolon landed on the cobbledstone ahead of him with a meaty thud. Ivan gripped his sword with fear.

"I know you," the monster said. "I knocked you from the wall in the Old City and left you for dead, didn't I? You sniveling, impotent coward. You're going to wish I had killed you that day." The muscled beast's growl resonated deeply in its barreled chest and its ivory mane prickled with rage. Rank saliva dripped from its jaws.

"My King." Terror tingled up Ivan's spine. "Come back. Help me."

The King appeared again, seemingly out of thin air. He ignored the diabolos. "I never left."

"I couldn't see you." Ivan quailed with fear.

"Like now, you mean?" The King vanished again. "See? You can still hear me. That's because I'm right here. Now do as I say."

As the King spoke the diabolos lowered its head and stepped forward, opening its jaws wider than Ivan thought possible. "I will devour you, Old City dweller, you faithless, foolish failure!"

It was true. He was a failure. Just like the knight killed beside him in the Old City. But he didn't want to die. Ivan's arms felt useless and his sword dragged like an anvil in his hands. Without help, he would certainly perish. "My Lord and King, I beg you. Show me how to fight."

"You don't have to fight."

The words were in his mind now, resonating powerfully in his soul. They were every bit as clear as they had been when the King had been standing right next to him. In fact, they sounded exactly the same as the audible voice had.

"I'm right next to you." The King read his thoughts. "Remember? I have defeated the creature before you. And I am within you."

"Which means I have defeated the diabolos too," Ivan said aloud, finishing the King's thought. The monster froze for a moment, a wave of fear rippling its way across the feral face. Then it took a step forward, howling like a red-hot kettle.

"I have nothing to fear." Ivan inhaled confidence from his invisible King. The thing took another step closer. Now its savage face was just inches from his own. He could smell its sulphuric breath as it opened its mouth wide again, exposing a tight mouthful of daggers. It trembled with bloodlust.

"Just use my name," the King spoke into his mind. "Lay down the law, Ivan." At those words, courage and righteous anger surged through him, like he'd been plugged into a powerful current of ennobling electricity.

"I am a servant son of the King of kings." Ivan's chest swelled with power.

"You don't have to raise your voice."

"Sorry." Ivan looked the diabolos straight in the eyes. "In the name of the King, step down."

"I am a free choosing being like you are. I can disobey you if I like." The beast snarled again, but Ivan noticed its rage melting under a mounting fear.

"Take that up with the King."

The diabolos blinked, confused by Ivan's courage. It retreated half a step. "You're a spineless fool. You're nothing." The words were empty and Ivan knew it. Even more importantly, the beast knew that he knew it.

"Be quiet." The lion's mouth snapped shut as if it had been caught in an invisible vice. "Leave me now, or face the judgment of the King." The thing scrambled backward, clawing the ground as if it were skating on ice. Ivan watched with disbelief as the massive head of the diabolos was dragged into fealty by the millstone of submission. Then it flapped its reptilian wings and shot into the air. A second later, it was gone.

"How did I … we … do that?" Ivan's heart was pounding. He looked around for the King again. Force of habit.

"Authority trumps power in Basileia." The King could not be seen but was obviously still present. "Even though they are greater than you and have fearsome strength, under my victory they are like chaff in the wind. They will tempt you to make such encounters about power. If you give in to that temptation, you cannot win. But if you refuse the bait, standing in my authority, you cannot lose. And you are still seeing them like they want you to see them." Ivan felt the King's invisible hands settle on his head. A vibrating sensation rippled through his skull.

"In the Old City people think that I'm at war with Pythus and his diabolon. But I have already defeated the dark ones. My war is over, or I could have no authority over them."

"But there is a war. I've seen it."

"Of course there is. With you. War is a contest of power, and with me there is no contest. Knowing this, Pythus has turned all his fury on the ones I love. On you. He yearns to defeat my children to spite me for humiliating him at the battle of the bridge."

"You said that I don't have to fight him, but in the Old City I saw people seriously hurt and even killed in battle."

"Of course. Remember how the Book of Life becomes to you what you think it's for? If you treat the diabolon as foes to be fought, they will happily indulge you and you will endure many wounds and casualties. But if you deal with them as the defeated foes they are, they must submit to your authority. My authority. Behold your fearsome enemy."

The King suddenly reappeared. He gripped a thick iron chain in his hand. At the end of the chain sat a gaunt old lion with tattered wings. A diabolos? The King reached out and grabbed one of its paws. There were no claws. Next he pried open the thing's mouth. It complied without resistance. To Ivan's astonishment, it had no teeth either. "I have disarmed your enemy," the King explained. The creature was obviously afraid of both Ivan and the King, and would have taken flight if it hadn't been held in place by the King's hefty chain.

"Then what I saw earlier was a deception? An illusion?"

The King vanished again, along with the diabolos. "The dark ones are disarmed, but they still hold considerable power to deceive and intimidate. As you have experienced firsthand, they still have their roar. If you give in to fear, by that fear you will be devoured."

Ivan nodded, then cocked his head to one side. "Oh, my sword." Ivan scanned the ground for his weapon. "I must have dropped it."

"You didn't drop it."

"Then where did it go?"

The King chuckled, and Ivan's tongue tingled. "I put it in your mouth."

# Chapter Thirteen: Change

"Ivan, wake up."

Ivan stirred, expecting to find the playful Shelah at his bedside again. Or perhaps his own daughter. Groping around in the pitch-blackness, Ivan found that he was still in Vita's cottage. Part of him was relieved. His friends had become like family to him. But part of him was disappointed. For a moment he thought he had been transported home again. Sadness washed over him momentarily, but he steeled himself to it. He had given that dream to the King.

Ivan's eyes adjusted to the dim light. There was no one in the room with him. Not that he could see, anyway. But the King was there. "I'm awake. What's going on?"

"Come with me."

"Sure. Let me get dressed." Slipping out of bed, Ivan shuffled his leaden feet toward his clothes. His toes began to tingle. A second later they lost contact with the floor and joy surged through his heart. He was flying.

With that, Ivan spun around once and glided out the window, at peace with the shimmering gold air. He was being drawn toward the King. Giving himself up to the pull, he ascended higher and higher, rising until he hung like a graceful star two hundred feet above the city. A gentle breeze teased his skin, but he was strangely warm. It felt marvelous for his body to be weightless, much like his soul had felt the past few weeks. He could see the whole city from where he fluttered—Golgotha, the treasury, the shimmering streets, the temple, the home of his friends below. It was a truly magical moment.

"I've always dreamt of flying."

"I love you too."

Something felt off. Slightly odd. "This is a dream, isn't it?"

The King nodded.

"Aw, nuts."

"But it's a real dream. From my heart to yours."

"Thank you." Ivan sighed. Had it been a month since his nightmarish terrors at the spring of death?

"A month tomorrow. Do you like the New City?"

"I love it. I was made for this."

"Yes. And yet …"

"I still miss my family. My wife, my daughter, my home, my yard, my church family. Even my car." He shrugged his shoulders. "I'm sorry. I will accept your will for me."

"You're sorry? Whatever for? You should miss them all, perhaps minus the car." The King laughed, then grew serious. "Ivan, things are going to change tomorrow."

"Change?"

"Yes. And you must trust me. In some ways, everything will seem different. But in truth, nothing will be."

"But what …"

"Ivan, wake up!"

Bolting upright in a panic, Ivan found Shelah at his bedside. Shaking his head, he tried to shed the cobwebs tangling up his brain. Facing her ever-present grin, he decided to tell her about his dream.

"I was flying."

"My dream was riding a horse in a field of clover and flowers."

"*Your* dream?"

"The one the King gave me before everything changed but nothing did."

"You … you had one too?"

"Yup. A long time ago. But the King asked me to wake you. Come on." He took her hand, then slid out of bed. Shelah led him through the house past Rosa and Vita—who looked parentally concerned, though not overly worried. He wondered what was going on until she pushed open the screeching door. He gasped.

The shimmering air was gone. The rippling pavement had vanished. The city's glow had faded. Ivan felt like he had put his finger into an electric socket. And his chest felt different. His head buzzed with shock. The spring was gone. The diabolon were gone, the darkness of Kakos was gone. Everything around him looked so normal and plain. His stomach wrenched itself into a merciless knot.

"Ivan." Vita and Rosa had joined him outside.

His throat locked up, stuck on a sob too big to rise. "I can't. I can't go back. I hate that Old City. I can't live without the King. I can't."

"You don't have to," Vita said, embracing him. "Don't be afraid."

"Don't be afraid? How can you say that? Over the past few weeks I've been given everything my soul has ever ached for and now it's gone. It's not fair. Why do you get to keep all your blessings?"

"We don't, sweetheart," Rosa said. "None of us do."

"What?"

"It's true." Ivan saw the honesty radiating from Vita's eyes as usual. His heart sank like a stone.

"Then all of this wasn't real?"

"Oh, it was real. We all experienced the first few weeks of revelation like you did. But a day always comes when we have to walk by faith, not by sight."

"You mean none of you saw or heard all the things I saw the past few weeks?" He rubbed his jaw in disbelief.

"Not with our physical eyes and ears," Rosa explained. "But we experienced all of it in our hearts."

Ivan didn't understand. How was it possible? Mercifully, they let him fumble through the weight of the moment. It felt like a bomb had been dropped on his faith.

"It's all still here, Ivan."

Ivan gasped. The voice of the King, audible and rich and real. "King, what's happening to me? What's going on?"

"I'm taking you home, one step at a time." This time the voice was in his mind.

"Home? I thought I wasn't going home."

"I never said that. I just wanted you to be at home here before sending you back. Now you can draw the realities of Basileia into your old life."

"My old life? In the Old City?"

"No, your old life with your family, your job, your yard, and your car. You remember your car, don't you?"

Now Basileia itself was beginning to fade from view. Ivan felt a wave of profound sadness and a quivering childlike excitement at the same time. He wanted to stay with the King, to live in Basileia. The truth was, he wasn't sure he could ever feel at home in the earthly realm now, but the thought of seeing Monica and Sarah made his chest hurt with anticipation. The knot in his gut began to loosen.

A moment later he was standing like a stranger in his old neighborhood. The contemporary rooflines were taking shape. The medieval city was nowhere to be seen. In just a few moments it had been replaced by his house and the car in the driveway.

Looking beyond it, his heart skipped like a stone bounding across a glassy pond.

Vita, Rosa, and Shelah were standing on a porch just four houses down, arms folded across their chests, grinning from ear to ear, as if they had been waiting for this moment.

"What? Is this possible?"

"We're here, aren't we?"

Ivan charged like a teenage bull across all four yards, leaping over planters and dodging parked vehicles, not stopping until he had nearly tackled his old friends and wrapped his arms around all of them in a giant bear hug.

"What are you doing here? And your clothes. Look at you. You're not peasants anymore."

"We live here, silly." Shelah poked his ribs, giggling.

"What?"

Vita and Rosa were beaming. "We're those neighbors you never quite had the nerve to come and meet," Rosa said, scolding playfully.

"You kinda kept to yourself," Vita explained. "I found you curled up in the fetal position on your front steps the other day. You've been staying with us since then."

He thought about that. It made no sense. "But you live here? I thought you lived in Basileia!"

"We still do, Ivan. Don't you remember what the King said?"

"I said that my kingdom overlaps your world." It was the King's voice sounding inside him.

"You mean …"

"He means that the New City, the grace, the air, the spring, the cross, the treasury, all of it, is right here, waiting for you to embrace in this world. Your faith in the King brings them all home."

Home. The word meant so much more than it had a month ago.

"The diabolon and Kakos and the chasm and the bridge are here too." Shelah nodded vigorously, obviously pleased with her simple kind of wisdom.

"My Father and I never stop working to manifest the realities of Basileia on earth, in this realm," the King said. "In Basileia my desires are always reality, but on earth they conflict with the wills of a million others. In those glorious moments when my desires are welcomed from Basileia to earth through the faith of your heart, miracles happen. The dead are raised. The lame are healed. Lives change. The prisoners are set free. Basileia is built. My kingdom pours into this realm."

Ivan's head was spinning. "I think I need more faith."

"No, you don't," Shelah said, correcting him.

"She's right. A mustard seed's worth of faith is all I need from you," said the King.

Ivan gasped. It was true. He could suddenly feel it. Or not exactly feel. It was deeper than that. A profound knowing from the core of his being. Every lesson he had learned, every moment of the whole adventure—even in the Old City—had prepared him for his normal life here on earth. He was going to say "in the real world," but he realized that Basileia was the real world too. He almost said "at home," but Basileia had become home too—as normal and real as the buckling cement on his driveway. They were both real and home at the same time. The saying was true. Home really was where the heart is, and his heart was in both places. That was the lesson he had been given.

The next moment nearly knocked him over. Very simply, his brain finally caught up with his faith and it all came back to him—in his mind's eye, that is. He could feel the spring within him. He knew the King's presence. He heard his voice in his heart. He saw the shimmering, glorious air of the kingdom. He felt the grace beneath his feet and the riches of the King's treasury. It was all here, all real, all the time. Though his eyes couldn't see it, he knew it. And that knowing was more powerful than any feeling. Stronger than anything else on earth.

Vita put his hand on Ivan's shoulder. "Sometimes the King peels back the veil and gives us glimpses of the New City. But mostly, he just helps us remember the truth and live it out. The hard part is living with a foot in each realm, which means facing the constant tension between what we see by faith and what we see with our eyes."

"And doing that without losing heart," Rosa said, completing his thought.

"Yup. And one day we'll go live with him in Basileia forever." Shelah's eyes sparkled like her daddy's.

"Faith will become sight," the King said. "I can hardly wait for that day, Ivan. I'm already preparing a special place for you in my New City."

Ivan nodded, rubbing his eyes as if trying to wake up. "You know, I think I'm going to be okay." He would have kept blabbering but his reverie was interrupted by a silver minivan gliding down the street. *Honk. Honk.* It was Monica and Sarah.

And then it all came back to him. The girls had stepped out for the weekend to give him some space. The weekend? His whole adventure had taken just a few days?

"Time is my plaything," the King said.

Ivan laughed. "Works for me." He eyed the van as it pulled into the driveway. "May I?"

"What are you waiting for?"

Ivan bounded over to the van and nearly ripped the sliding door off its hinges. "Monica, honey, I met the King. I really did. I went to live in Basileia and I'm back now, and wow, do I have a story to tell you."

Monica looked at him blankly. "Basileia?"

"The kingdom of God."

"And you ... you ... went there?"

Ivan nodded, stilled by the solemnity of the moment. "I'm still there now. All three of us are, actually." He knew how foolish it all sounded, but he didn't care. It was the truth. His new reality.

"Right here? On the driveway?"

"Uh huh. Isn't it great?" He stomped his feet in excitement.

Monica tilted her head heavenward and began to laugh. Sarah leaned forward, trying to wiggle out of her car seat.

"What's so funny, Mommy? Daddy, why is Mommy laughing at you?"

They ignored her for the time being.

"Really, Ivan? Basileia?"

Ivan nodded.

Tears spilled over her eyelids, marking her cheeks with a ragged joy. Resting her forehead on the steering wheel, she whispered a heartfelt prayer.

"Thank you, King. Thank you."

# The End

# Epilogue

It's time to lower the curtain on Basileia, leaving joyful Ivan (me) bear-hugging his family on the driveway.

Where does that leave you? Maybe you resonate with the kingdom picture I've been painting. Maybe you're already living that kind of life. But perhaps not. Perhaps you're still wrestling with the concepts. Either way, I'm pretty sure I've made you think, and that's beautiful.

Personally speaking, I'm done living in the Old City—along with its soul-killing striving, seeking, thirsting, and fighting—praise God. I'm absolutely convinced that King Jesus opened up a new and living way for me through his death and resurrection. I'm increasingly experiencing that dynamic way of life—a path marked by loving, trusting, enjoying, and reigning. I'm learning to live with one foot in this world and another in Christ's wondrous kingdom—my true country—the eternal realm pulsing just beyond the veil of my senses. As you can tell, I'm never going back. I hope you come along for the ride if you haven't already.

Your perspective determines your experience. That's why I've deliberately taken aim at the way you see your faith, daring you to wrestle with the living collage of images, thoughts, and feelings of this parable. I hope I've evoked something, poked something, even choked something. I pray that your heart is having a personal apocalypse—a revelation of Christ that changes life as you know it.

As I said earlier, this manuscript is eight years in the making. My ideas are a work in progress, but as a friend of mine commented, likening this manuscript to a piece of art, "At some point you just have to sign your name to the work and call it done." I agree. My job is done. But the thing is, I've just lobbed the proverbial ball into your court. Now it's your turn. You've got to write yourself into the story and finish the tale in real life.

I'm guessing that at least some of you are asking good questions: "What about angels, or the routines of work or family or school? What about (fill in the blanks)?" And I get that. I know perfectly well that I haven't told the whole story or written a fully orbed manifesto of the Christian life. It's a parable, after all, and parables aren't supposed to nail everything down. We're trying to get away from "the old way of the written code," remember? My advice is to let *Finding Home* be what it is. It's only a parable, right?

Or is it?

Remember the toothless greeter at the city gate? His question still stands.

"Old City or New City?"

Brad Huebert,
April, 2008

Breinigsville, PA USA
13 December 2010

251277BV00002B/42/P